CATERED
TO
DEATH

ALSO BY LAURA PAULING

Murder with a Slice of Cheesecake
Footprints in the Frosting
Deadly Independence
Frosted on the Ferris Wheel
Fruitcake and Foul Play
Poison in the Pastry
Catered to Death
Pie Crust and Peril
Lemon Meringue and Murder
Coffee Cake and Clues
Tiramisu and Trouble

BARON & GRAYSTONE MYSTERIES

Caramel Macchiato Murder
Macadamia Fudge Murder
Chocolate Raspberry Murder
Pumpkin Spice Murder
Peppermint Mocha Murder

CATERED TO DEATH

Laura Pauling

Redpoint Press

Text copyright 2016 Laura Pauling
All rights reserved.

No part of this publication may be reproduced, stored in a retrieval system or transmitted in any form or by any means, electronic, or otherwise, without written permission from the publisher.
For information visit www.laurapauling.com

paperback ISBN 13: 978-1523725939
paperback ISBN 10: 1523725931

Summary: Holly's past resurfaces in the form of a childhood friend--and a murder. Is Holly next?

Edited by Cindy Davis

for all mystery lovers

1

IT HAD TO BE six o'clock in the morning. Had to be. Holly blinked at the sunshine streaming through her bedroom. Normally, this would bring a smile, or at least the start of one, but she didn't want to face another day of Millicent popping into her life with a wink and a laugh—like she'd never been blackmailing Holly. Like they hadn't been frenemies for the past year.

Holly disliked giving in to Millicent's demands, but ever since Holly dropped the hint her family had connections to the publishing industry, Millicent had gone overboard the other direction. The latest stunt had been a copy of her book's dedication.

This book is dedicated to my best friend, Holly. Without her by my side through thick and thin this book never would've been written. Without her wisdom and keen insight into human nature you wouldn't be about to read the most mysterious mystery novel ever. She inspires everyone she meets to be a better person...

Holly crumpled the paper and threw it on the floor. The dedication went on for another four paragraphs. Four!

Muffins yipped and barked, racing into her bedroom. He leaped onto the bed and tugged at her pajama tops.

"What in the world has gotten into you?" She glanced at the clock. Yikes! Nine o'clock, not the crack of dawn.

He continued to nip and pull at her pajamas, raced to the door, and then back to the bed.

"I get the message. You need to pee. You're hungry. And you want your walk." She could just slip outside with him. No one would notice a neighbor in pajamas, right? Even if they did, by this time, months later, Holly realized no one cared. It was practically normal for a small town. Well, maybe not normal, but not something anyone would snub their noses at or look on her with judgment.

"Fine. Fine. Let's go," she grumbled, shuffling to the kitchen. By habit, she grabbed the leash and hooked it onto his collar.

He pawed the door. Then raced to the window and back to the door.

"Coming, coming." She slipped into flip-flops, grateful the long winter was over. The warmth of spring was more than welcome to thaw everything out.

He ran back to the window, so Holly followed. Across the street, Millicent stood in the parking lot wearing a short skirt, a turquoise shirt, and a bright scarf. Ugh.

"Let's go, Muffins."

Muffins practically dragged her down the stairs from her second-story apartment. He wanted to head to the front and pulled on his leash.

Even if the town might not care about frog pajamas—cutest, softest jammies in the country, possibly the world—she didn't necessarily want to parade around town in them. "To the back," she ordered and forced Muffins to the tiny backyard to take care of business. "We'll walk later."

While Muffins sniffed around in the grass, Holly thought about the coming days, the coming weeks, and the rest of the year. She wasn't sure if she could handle too much more of Millicent. In the past month, since their little conversation, she'd left freshly baked muffins at Holly's door and offered to scrub her kitchen floor. Her latest gift had been a gift card for a year of free coffee at *The Tasty Bite*.

Holly felt the tug and the slight burn of the leash ripping from her hand when Muffins took off, sprinting to the front.

"Get back here!" That dog. She'd let her guard down, lost in her thoughts. Somehow, he'd known, waiting. He was way too smart.

She gave chase, almost slipping in the dew-wet grass. In the front, he stood, his gaze focused. Holly looked across the street, gasped, and then dove behind the hedges. She landed in the newly laid mulch and didn't care. Panic prickled and raced across her skin. Her shallow breaths sounded in her ears as did her pounding heart.

She didn't dare look again. Couldn't. This couldn't be happening.

Muffins rested his head on her lap. She leaned against the building. After a few seconds, he nipped at her arm as if to tell her she couldn't hide behind the hedges forever. Why not though? Trent and Charlene would surely drop off meals and provide her with books to pass the time. They might even camp out with her.

She had to double check.

On her knees, she inched to the edge and poked her head around the side. It was him.

Teddy. Her childhood friend.

The dark hair that flopped on his forehead. His teeth gleamed in the morning sun—or was it her imagination? As usual, he was dressed in a dapper suit, like he was heading into a meeting with the president. She pulled back and took a few deep breaths. That sort of thing helps panic attacks, right?

Curiosity and self-preservation motivated her to look once more. A bit calmer, she noticed the way Millicent flirted with him. After all, she was a professional. If flirting were an Olympic event, she'd win a gold medal. The brief touch on his arm. The invasion of personal space. The gaze into his eyes. Holly imagined the low, seductive voice, the high-pitched giggle, accompanied by the furious batting of the eyelashes. Holly wanted to barf right there in the hedges.

Millicent didn't have to beg to get men's attention. Within seconds, she had Teddy wrapped around her finger.

They walked into *Oodles* together, probably for a brunch date.

Why was Teddy in Fairview?

In one rush, all the memories returned. Of the last few weeks with her parents before she moved. Her Aunt Lizzie, murdered by her parents' business partners—Teddy's parents. The crime covered up by the local cop, Chief Harrison. And then, Teddy, abducting her, clearly in on the whole thing.

And now, somehow, he'd found her. Or maybe this was a complete coincidence. Maybe he was just out for a friendly drive. Two hours away from home. Right. Teddy never did anything for fun and relaxation.

Millicent. Holly hissed out a breath. Had the past month been an act while behind the sugary smile and gifts, she'd been scheming? Had she gone so far as to contact Teddy? Was her next move to flaunt him in front of her and then, reinstate the blackmail, force her to close shop and move from Fairview? To be honest, at this point, that idea was appealing. She'd forget everything, and maybe, her heartache would fade into nothing. Eventually.

She didn't plan or scheme. She grabbed Muffins into a football hold and sprinted across the street. Without a second thought, she sat at an outside table next to the window. She received a few odd looks, but she didn't care. She knew exactly the table where Millicent loved to sit inside.

A minute or so later, her sugary voice drifted out the window. "So do you need someone to show you around town? I've lived here forever"—she cackled—"I mean, not forever, I'm probably your age. I grew up here. I know all the best spots. The best shops, the hiking trails, the best view points."

Holly bit back a snort. View points. Millicent probably did know all the romantic spots. She'd probably dragged Trent to enough of them.

"Would you like to start with a drink order? Miss?"

The waitress. Holly was sitting at a table. In her pajamas. But she couldn't speak or they'd hear her. She shook her head.

"Are you ready to order then?" the waitress asked.

Holly yanked open the menu and shook her head again.

The waitress flashed her a smile. "I'll be back in a few minutes. Take your time."

Holly focused on the conversation inside. What had she missed?

Millicent was babbling again. "What? You've heard about some famous cheesecake from this little ole town? You must mean my father's then. He makes the best. It's unbeatable."

Holly seethed, wishing down curses of bad kissing and bad breath on Millicent for the coming years.

Then a familiar voice, deep and friendly, pierced her heart while at the same causing her to shudder. "Actually, I know the name. *Just Cheesecake*, I believe? Have you heard of it? I've been searching the surrounding small towns for it."

That was all Holly needed to hear.

He was looking for her. His appearance in Fairview wasn't a coincidence or the result of a scenic drive. Somehow, her secret was out. He probably wanted to kill her. Sent to snuff her out because she was a loose thread. Or use her as bait to pull her parents out of hiding.

Someone whispered in her ear. "Spying, are we?"

HOLLY STARTLED AND LET out a squeak. She slapped her hand over her mouth. Trent crouched at her side. Had Teddy heard? Had Millicent? She'd recognize Trent's voice and probably be making a mad dash for the door right now. Holly held her breath, listening.

They'd stopped talking.

With an I-can't-believe-you glare at Trent, she tightened her grip around Muffins and hurried past the windows, crouched over like a ninety-year-old man. Once she hit the sidewalk, she went into an all-out sprint. She couldn't cross the street, because Millicent or Teddy might look out the window.

She kept running. Her lungs screamed and a cramp pierced her side.

"Holly!"

Trent was chasing her. Oh, crap. Had Teddy heard? She stopped mid-sprint and stumbled. He couldn't call her name again. She whirled around almost slamming into Trent.

"Hey, I was just joking." He eyed her crazy appearance, dirt-stained pajamas, bed head, and wild eyes.

One glance beyond his shoulder revealed Millicent and Teddy entering the parking lot. Only a hundred feet away. Sprinting would cause a distraction, and she definitely couldn't stay and chat. Without another look at Trent, she cut through a yard and a small business parking lot until she exited onto a side street. Only then did she allow herself to slow and catch her breath.

"Holly?"

He was still following her. She had to lie. "Sorry about that. But no, I wasn't spying. Those days are done. I got locked out of the apartment again after Muffins ran away. Stupidly, I decided to eat breakfast at *Oodles* until I could reach my landlord when I realized I had no money..."

"And then you decided to train for a marathon?"

Of course, he knew she was lying. Of course, he knew something was wrong. Of course. Of course. Of course.

"Actually, you're right. It must be the spring air, but I decided, just in that moment before eating, that I'd gained a few pounds and training for a marathon or at least attempting to jog was the thing for me."

He stared. Not in a mean or cold or interrogating kind of way. More like in an I-know-you kind of way. An I-know-something-is-wrong kind of way.

She could tell Trent about Teddy. She'd already shared her past with him when Millicent was blackmailing her.

"Is Millicent attempting to blackmail you again?" he asked. Acting ready to chase her down and cuff her if that was the case.

"Pfft. I wish." Anything would be better than more bloated novel dedications. A part of her didn't want to say Teddy's name out loud, because that would make it real. But this was Trent. "Teddy," she whispered. "I saw Teddy."

Trent stiffened. "Where?" He scoped the surrounding neighborhood as if Teddy had followed them. "Here in Fairview?"

Holly nodded. "He was eating with Millicent."

A beep sounded at Trent's waist—the station. He had to respond. He ignored it and pulled her into a hug.

The beep sounded again.

"You've got to go." Holly pushed him away. "Don't want Chief Hardy breathing down your neck."

He grasped her hand. "We'll talk later. Okay? Make a plan. Call in the mystery club. Inquire about the witness protection program. Something."

She smiled. "Thank you. We'll talk later."

He paused. "You won't do anything stupid, will you? Nothing rash or spur-of-the-moment?"

Holly laughed. "Of course not."

***

AN HOUR LATER, AFTER wandering streets and taking the long route around, in her pajamas, tired and sweaty and face streaked with pure panic tears, Holly arrived home.

On automatic, she fed Muffins, closed all the curtains, then jumped in the shower. With wet hair, Holly sat in front of her computer and Googled Teddy.

The first article that popped up was an interview. His concerned face took up half the page. Holly cringed. He talked about the recent rash of robberies in their neighborhood. He talked about running for mayor. He talked about cold crimes and Aunt Lizzie and the Hartfords.

Holly gasped. Why would he mention her family? Why, after one year, would he bring up Aunt Lizzie? She read on.

In a few well-written and suave paragraphs, he highlighted her family as possibly being responsible for the robberies. That after being suspect in a long-term scheme to embezzle money from their company, her parents and had left town with nothing. Their daughter, possibly connected to the family murder, as she most likely needed funds, was also at large, and could possibly have returned to steal from her previous neighbors. Desperate. Guilty. And not in her right mind.

Holly seethed. She screamed. She pounded her fist on the table, quickly regretting it when pain radiated up her arm. She wanted to smash the screen. How dare he?

Maybe it was Muffins, who sat obediently at her feet. Maybe she was slightly out of her right mind. Maybe it the lingering close contact with Trent, but something shifted.

This wasn't going to stop.

Obviously, Teddy had grabbed the bull by the horns. No, he'd thrown the bull down with his bare hands. Teddy wanted her. Or...he wanted something. But what? If his parents were truly guilty of embezzling funds from companies over the years—not her family—why would he want her parents back in the picture? He was clearly working for his parents. They had the local cop in their pockets. With Teddy as mayor, they'd have an inside road to the local government.

If this wasn't going to stop, then Holly would take action. To protect herself. To protect her family. The memories and desire for justice for Aunt Lizzie welled. Solving murders in the past year helped quench that desire for justice. But maybe she'd fooled herself and it was more like sprinkling a few drops of water on wilting flowers.

"Let's go, Muffins. Time for a road trip."

He whimpered as if to remind her she was already late opening the shop.

She tapped his nose. "That's one good thing about running your own business. Personal days."

She changed into all black clothing, not entirely sure why because she'd be breaking into her parents' house during the light of day. She packed food and her sharpest cooking knife—just in case. Drawing as little attention as possible, she carried Muffins and her stuff to the car and pulled onto Main Street. In minutes, she was driving the back roads to her parents' house.

It only took two hours but it felt like thirty minutes when she pulled into the nearest park. Kids were in school so the jungle gym equipment looked empty and sad. The tennis courts were bare. The soccer fields overgrown. It was the perfect place to leave the car. It wasn't like she could park in her driveway.

She didn't dare leave Muffins in the car. Her parents had told her he was sensitive to danger and loyal to her. This morning, he'd known Teddy was in town. He'd alerted her to his presence. "You're not leaving my side, buddy."

Then she started on the trails that would eventually border the woods behind her parents' home. The trail was on the muddy side from winter and in need of trimming, so it was slower going. She ducked tree branches, not always missing them. She swatted mosquitoes. But none of it really bothered her.

She was more focused and more driven than she'd been in weeks.

Near her parents' backyard, she completed a perimeter check, then studied the house. No, more like a mansion. She'd forgotten. About living with so much. About privilege.

About wanting for nothing. And she didn't miss it one bit. Holly missed her friends and she missed Trent.

A twig snapped behind her in the woods.

Terrified, she whirled and peered through the branches and weedy trail. It didn't take long to spot the source of the noise attempting to hide behind a skinny birch tree.

She huffed. "I see you, Millicent." This was so not what she needed. She'd have to pander to Millicent's curiosity and questions.

Unashamedly, Millicent stepped out and closed the gap between them. "I knew you were up to something when you sneaked out dressed in black. I was right."

In three seconds, Holly made a decision. "Fine. I'm checking on my parents' house. I read about robberies in the area."

"Sure. Whatever you say." She tucked her short blonde hair behind her ears. "I'll play along with that. I wished I'd dressed differently."

"Just follow and don't touch anything."

As a precaution, Holly pulled up her hood to hide her telltale red hair and sprinted across the yard. She felt silly. No one was watching. It was her home. Why did she feel guilty?

She had the key and could enter through the door. She was about to climb the steps of the back porch when she noticed the smashed window.

Millicent spoke behind her. "The remains of the shattered window gleamed in the sun, sharp and jagged. Someone had broken into the house."

"It's cloudy," Holly pointed out. "And can you stop the whole recorder thing?"

Millicent sniffed. "We might want the details later."

The broken window did appear to be a break in. Fear, real fear, snaked through her veins. They had a security system. Had they been robbed? Teddy had mentioned the rash of burglaries. And no one lived here. Professionals would know how to circumvent the alarm system.

She expected their house to be stripped of electronics. That would be the fastest and the easiest. But when she entered the pass code and unlocked the door, she was caught off guard.

The place was trashed.

Millicent spoke into her recorder. "This looked like more than the normal robbery. Every thing had been overturned and emptied. Complete devastation."

Holly gripped Muffins and patted his head, more for her comfort. The destruction took her breath away. Every dish and glass had been heaved from the cupboards. Even the china and the crystal. All worth money. Muffins whimpered.

"Sorry, buddy. I don't want you to step on anything sharp." She picked her way through the mess into the living room, Millicent right behind her. Again, everything was pulled apart, but the flat screen TV still in place. Glass crunched underfoot as she made her way down the hall to her father's office.

A gasp escaped.

All her dad's files covered the floor, a messy paper trail that made one thing glaringly obvious. She didn't need to be a cop or trained in anything. This wasn't an innocent robbery. And whoever did this—her mind immediately thought of Teddy and his family whether they did the dirty work or not—wasn't looking for money or valuables.

"Did you have to break all the china?" That was mean spirited. They wanted information. Possibly records. The question remained—did they find what they'd wanted?

Maybe it was time to contact her parents, or the family's lawyer, Senior Rumford. Certainly, he would have timely words of wisdom before she freaked out. In fact, he probably knew more about the robberies than her. Unfortunately, her parents had wanted to protect her from the fact they'd been working undercover to expose Teddy's family as embezzlers, rich on stolen money. They only told her minutes before they all went into hiding, and then she moved to her new life in Fairview. She realized how little she knew, because for the last year she'd been running in an attempt to forget.

"Secrets littered the room in the form of files and papers and memos. This was no ordinary break-in and—"

Someone moaned.

Millicent gripped Holly's arm. "Did you hear that?"

"Yes."

The moan came again.

Holding her breath, dread slithering into her gut, she left her dad's office and followed the sound. At the doorway of the great room where her parents held their grand parties, she found the source.

A man lay crumpled on the floor, blood pooled under his body.

Senior Rumford.

3

For what seemed like an hour, Holly could only stare. She'd stumbled upon many bodies, starting with Aunt Lizzie. Somehow, this was different. More ghastly.

"Do you know him?" Millicent whispered.

"Rumford," she gasped out, thinking of his wife and family. She barely made it across the room to kneel by him. She pressed two fingers to his neck. Nothing at first, and then...a pulse. Slow, but there.

"Should I call 911?"

"No. Not yet."

"Why not?"

"Because. Just let me think." She couldn't think about anything but saving Rumford.

She raced back to the kitchen, grabbed towels, and raced back. Stop the blood. She knew that much. Fighting the gag reflex, she pressed towels against what looked like a knife wound. Not good.

"Don't just stand there! Get more towels!" Holly barked at Millicent, who stood, pale and shaking in the doorway, for the first time, not speaking into the recorder.

"Senior Rumford?" Holly hoped he was still somewhat conscious. No answer. As she sat, with hands pressed to this man's chest, thoughts shot through her mind in rapid succession. She couldn't leave him here to die. She couldn't reveal herself. It would destroy everything. She thought about calling Trent. About calling Charlene. Her parents.

He groaned again.

Millicent arrived back, breathless, and dropped dishtowels by Holly's side. "We have to do something."

"I know." Holly didn't have the medical training to know what to do. They had to save his life. Regardless of the consequences. With one hand pressed against the towel, she fumbled for her phone to realize she'd left it home.

He hissed her name. His eyes blinked open.

Millicent screamed and dropped her phone into the pool of blood.

"Senior Rumford. What happened? Who did this to you? Why here?" Then the questions flooded her brain. Why here? What was he doing in her house? Were they following him? Were they still here? She froze, panic simmering.

"Holly..." he hissed. His mouth opened and shut as he tried to talk.

"Don't try. Let me call the ambulance." She glanced at Millicent's phone in the blood. "Do you have a phone? Um, ours isn't going to work." She searched his jacket for inside pockets.

He grabbed her wrist.

"No." He gasped and wheezed.

Then a breath hissed out and there wasn't another one.

"No!" She wiped at her face.

If she called the local police—she shuddered at the memory of Chief Harrison—it would be like alerting Teddy and his family to her presence. In fact, she'd probably be found guilty. She glanced around. Her prints would be all over the scene.

"Come on." Millicent tugged on Holly's arm. "Let's get out of here. I don't have a good feeling."

Adrenaline running, shock penetrating her body, Holly ran back to the kitchen and picked up the phone. Trent would know what to do, regardless. She slammed it back down. No service.

"Holly! We have to leave."

What next? She was frozen with indecision, her vision blurred temporarily. Then she refocused and looked at the counter for the first time. When she'd run through earlier, she'd been too much in shock to notice small details. What must be the murder weapon, their sharpest knife, lay on the counter, along with some of her dad's effects.

No way. Her dad would never…

Not for one second did Holly think her father had anything to do with this. No, her family was being framed. Immediately, she thought about Teddy's well-thought-out and well-timed comments in the newspaper. If he were spreading rumors about her family then the town, the people, even the neighborhood would believe her father of murder.

There was only one thing to do.

She had to hide the body.

In a normal murder situation like this, especially with the window of her house broken, she wouldn't be charged or suspect. But this was Teddy. The guy who had the chief of police in his back pocket. She couldn't chance it.

Pushing aside the grief and the shock, she went to the kitchen sink and scrubbed the blood off her hands. She didn't know where, but she'd store the body. She wouldn't let her family be destroyed over this. Then, she'd figure out a way to reveal Teddy and his family.

"You've lost it, Holly Hart. I realize this is a traumatic experience and you're probably feeling shock and indecision. This is quite common and not something to be scared of. We should wipe our prints and leave everything as is. We'll find a phone and leave an anonymous call at the police station."

Millicent kept rambling, but Holly didn't hear one word.

On her way out, she relocked the door to the house and then sprinted back to the car.

"Holly, wait! Darn these high-heeled boots," Millicent muttered.

Holly tripped over roots and wasn't as careful picking her way through the trails, so she came out with more scratches from overgrown branches. At the car, out of breath, she leaned against it. It had to be fast. She'd have to drive the car up the driveway, circle back around behind the house, and drag the body to her car. She couldn't think about the body as Senior Rumford, close family friend. She couldn't think about all the times his family had dined at their home, laughing and joking.

Justice. It burned inside her, spreading like a forest fire through her veins. She'd drive around and then return at night. No. They probably had it planned to "discover" the body, probably during a friendly neighborhood watch. She didn't know exactly how they worked, but she was positive Teddy would encourage tactics considered more invasive.

It had to be done now.

Millicent, out of breath, leaned against the car. "Now I know you've lost it. What do you want to do? I suggest we do nothing. Think about it. Call a meeting of the mystery club."

Her face set, Holly turned to Millicent. "You can come with me or leave." She pointed to Millicent's car parked behind hers. "It's up to you. I won't hold it against you if you don't want to help."

"Um, help with what?"

"Hiding the body."

Millicent squeaked but climbed into the passenger side. "I'm in."

Holly drove back to the house. No one should recognize her beat-up, four-door car that her family had provided so no one would notice her. Determined, she pulled into the long, winding driveway. At the top—thankfully it was hidden from the main road—she gunned the engine and veered off the driveway, over the side yard and through her mom's treasured landscaping.

"Sorry, Mom," she whispered.

All the technical aspects of what she was about to attempt flooded through her. What else could she do?

Almost separating herself from what her body was doing, she grabbed plastic trash bags from under the sink. As she and Millicent spread them in the trunk all she could think about was that this felt like some crazy movie. She almost let out a laugh. Almost.

When the plan formed, it scared her how easily it came. Back in the great room, she laid her mother's favorite blanket from their couch next to the body. "Okay, let's roll him onto it."

Trying not to look and after closing his eyes, they heaved him over onto the blanket. "You carry the blanket by the feet. I'll take the head." They lifted the body. It was slow going. Did she have that much time? When would the neighborhood watch arrive?

Hopefully, they'd find nothing wrong. Or when the real murderer arrived, they'd be dumbfounded at the missing body. Their plans gone awry.

On the porch, Millicent lost her hold, and the body bumped onto the porch.

"Sorry!"

Holly cringed. "Sorry, Mr. Rumford."

Muffins yipped from the front seat of the car. Was he warning her of danger? Was someone arriving out front?

She had to know.

Half out of her mind, she sprinted to the side and peeked to the front and the driveway. Sure enough, a few old ladies from the neighborhood with what looked like Stop Crime badges were getting out of a car.

Racing back, she entered through back door, again. Grabbing another blanket, she threw it over the blood, now soaked into the carpet. Hopefully they wouldn't check the back. In the kitchen, she grabbed another trash bag and shoveled in everything off the counter, hoping she got all the evidence against her dad. On the way out, she relocked the door.

After throwing the bag in the back, she said, "In the trunk."

Somehow, within the span of a few minutes, they managed to lift the body into the car. Adrenaline provided the energy. Okay, so a few times Senior Rumford hit the ground and the bumper, but they did it. Then she checked to make sure no blood smears remained on the bumper. They were good.

"Stay here." Holly raced back through the landscaping she'd trampled in her car. And listened.

"I don't know why we check here every week. The Hartfords haven't been back, and probably won't be coming back."

"Especially if they're guilty of everything."

"You heard what he said though. Check the entire house."

Holly held her breath and crossed her fingers, praying they'd be lazy. She didn't have any question who they were referring to. Had to be Teddy. She listened, cringing, as the women argued about how thorough they should be every time.

"Oh, you just want to impress Chief Harrison, seeing as you've had a crush on him for years."

"I do not. I say we look through the windows and if nothing is amiss, we head out. I'm hungry. There's a two-for-one special at Denny's."

The one lady was determined though. "Nope. We're doing the whole thing."

Holly sprinted back to the car. She slipped inside, fingers on the key. As soon as they came around, she'd gun it and escape.

She pulled the hood over her head and tucked all her hair into the back. Hopefully, they wouldn't know if she was male or female. She waited, sweat creeping down her back. Hyper focused and ready, she stared at the side of the house, waiting for them to come around the corner.

4

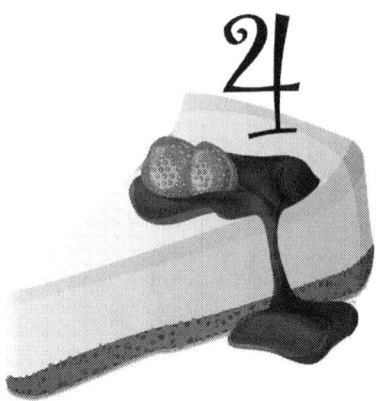

A minute went by. Then two. Then three.

And ten.

A car revved, and then, slowly, the sound of the engine faded. The neighborhood watch had left.

Finally, she sagged, letting her head drop to the wheel. Her body shook. She thought about her parents as the tears formed. The entire last year had been nothing but make believe. Maybe Millicent was right.

Holly was nothing but a fake.

"Um," Millicent said, "I hate to interrupt what I'm sure are intelligent plans for this ridiculous idea to hide the body, but I think we should get out of here."

Holly shook off the thoughts. Millicent was right. They had to get out of there before anyone else arrived. So Holly drove. She drove back over the landscaping, across the yard, and down the driveway. At the bottom, she turned right. She couldn't go straight back to Fairview. Until she had a plan.

She had a body in her trunk. A dead body.

"When I'm gone, you can have my original edition Nancy Drew collection."

Millicent gasped. "Do you know how much those are worth?" She quickly recovered. "Not that I'd ever sell them so who cares. Right? Right."

"Let Charlene know she can keep Muffins. She'll take good care of him."

"Definitely. Anything else?"

Holly let out a shaky breath. "Not really. I guess you'll have another shot with Trent, and your dad will have to take care of the cheesecake customers in Fairview."

Silence fell between them. It wasn't a relaxed, calm silence. Holly white-knuckled the steering wheel, only swerving off the road three times. Millicent pressed her foot against the floor of the car as if she could slow it down.

"Okay, I've been playing along with you, but this is ridiculous. It's not like this Teddy guy is going to jump out of the darkness and kill you."

"You don't know Teddy." She offered Millicent a grim look. "He's good at presentation." She relaxed her grip. "Anyway, I'm thinking of the time I'll be sentenced."

"What? That's ridiculous. You've done nothing wrong."

Holly's fragile emotions cracked. "Nothing wrong? I left a crime scene and never reported it. That will mean prison for decades right there."

"Pfft. I doubt it. You're being dramatic."

"Dramatic? Like I said, you don't know Teddy. You didn't read the articles where he placed full blame on me and my family, making us sound desperate. He has the whole town eating from his hand. They'll believe anything." Holly couldn't stop talking. "Never mind that he's running for mayor and has the town cops in his back pocket. Nope. I'm definitely donning orange in my near future."

Millicent laughed. "Don't forget about the body."

"How could I forget?" She giggled too.

They paused, glancing at each other, realizing that it was completely inappropriate to laugh and there wasn't anything funny about the current situation. Then they burst out laughing.

When sirens sounded behind them, the laughter died. For the first time, she realized how she looked. Bloodstained shirt. She pulled over and closed her eyes.

"We're going to die. I just know it. I'll be all over the news and my chances at a publishing deal will be ruined," Millicent muttered.

This was it. Everything was over.

Sirens blaring, the cruiser passed and sped out of sight.

With a gasp, Holly leaned her head against the back of the seat. She had to get off the road. "Let's stop somewhere and talk this through. Maybe wash up."

"I didn't want to point this out, because I thought you might be ready to snap, but I need my car."

Holly drove back and dropped Millicent off. "Follow me."

At the first small, run-down, no-name motel, they checked in. Millicent babbled about a cooking contest they returned from and how cherry stains never come out. The man behind the desk, with a thin mustache that probably never grew in, tossed her the key.

In the room, the wallpaper out of date and fading, the smell musty but clean, she flopped on the bed. The room key and car keys were clutched in her hand. Millicent lay down next to her.

"So who would be after this guy?" Millicent asked.

"Teddy and his family." But why? Just to pull Holly and her family from hiding? Or was there more? "Other than that, I don't know."

Holly had no idea what Rumford had been about to tell her before he died. She didn't think about it long though when exhaustion stole over her, and she slept. She startled awake hours later, dusk creeping through the window. The body. Rumford. She jerked up, wheezing.

"Calm down," Millicent ordered. "We're in a motel. We came from the crime scene. And you've been sleeping for hours."

Hours? She cringed. Was the body already decomposing?

"Thankfully, I had the wits about me to stay awake and brainstorm ideas on how to dispose of the body."

"That sounds so…cold."

Millicent glared. "We could always just drive it to the police station then."

"Fine. What are your ideas?" Holly sat and rubbed the sleep from her eyes.

"Tie a cement block to his feet and throw him in a river. Burn it. Bury it at least ten feet underground." Millicent ticked off her list.

It was a ridiculous list. They needed the body. To use against Teddy. That meant they needed to preserve it. "I know."

"What?" Millicent sighed.

"We'll freeze him."

***

HOLLY AND MILLICENT SCRUBBED the blood the best they could from their bodies. Holly turned her shirt inside out. Why hadn't she brought extra clothes?

Because she never expected to find a body.

They made the drive back to Fairview. By the time she pulled into *Just Cheesecake*, it was dark.

"If I didn't say it before," Millicent said, "I think your plan is brilliant."

Holly laughed. "You're just buttering me up so I'll send your manuscript to an editor."

"Ha! Your family is riddled with scandal. I'm not placing much faith in that anymore."

"Very true." Holly scanned the lot. Someone was peering in the windows of *Just Cheesecake*. "Who's that?" But she knew. After years of knowing someone, it's easy to pick out the way they walk, move, and peek into windows.

"It's Teddy, isn't it?"

"Yup."

"Man, why do the hotties have to be the bad guys…or taken?"

"World's biggest unsolved mystery," Holly said. Millicent still looked perfect, despite their afternoon activities. "Ready to put your flirting skills to the test?"

"What?" Millicent clutched her chest. "Are you proposing that I use my feminine charm to distract the murderer? Rather dangerous, don't you think?"

"Not for you. Not really. You work on him, and I'll hide the body."

"Deal." Millicent climbed out of the car and sauntered toward Teddy.

Holly parked the car behind the shops. She went inside and pulled all the recent cheesecakes, bars, and cookies she'd made that were in the freezer and crammed them into the shelves. Time for a half-off sale. Tomorrow.

She studied the freezer. It would have do. Anywhere else and decay would settle in. Hopefully, this would keep any evidence intact too. This was the only option until she figured out who murdered Rumford. Or how to prove Teddy and his family were behind it.

Cringing and whispering apologies to Mr. Rumford and his family, she brought out the dolly she used to move heavy deliveries. Somehow, she managed to get Rumford—no, the body—onto the dolly and inside. Shadows cloaked her movement, yet she braced any moment for someone to see her. In a small town, it could happen.

Inside *Just Cheesecake* she tipped the dolly and pushed the "delivery" into the upright freezer. Obviously, he couldn't stand, so Holly had to settle for nudging his limbs back inside when they flopped out. She winced every time. When she got it closed, she used the padlock. Then she slumped against the door.

All she wanted was a hot bath and a glass of wine.

Outside, before leaving, she glanced at the shop. She loved this little place and her business and this town.

Voices sounded from the front of the store, heading her way. She recognized Teddy and Millicent. Impulsively, she stepped into the shadows against the back wall of the store. Millicent and Teddy drew closer.

"The owner should probably be around tomorrow. Though, I promise I can provide much more decadent cheesecakes."

"Thanks for the offer, but my mother insisted upon *Just Cheesecake*. One of her friends had been through last summer and highly recommended them."

Millicent mumbled something that Holly couldn't hear. They were drawing closer.

"Come on," Millicent cooed. "Let's grab a nightcap, and then I'll bring you around tomorrow afternoon."

"Fine." Teddy's voice sounded tight and controlled. Holly barely recognized him as her childhood friend. She never thought she'd appreciate Millicent's influence over men.

When their footsteps faded, Holly sagged, her ragged breathing piercing the air.

Seconds turned into minutes.

She grabbed Muffins from the car, ran across Main Street, and sprinted up the steps to her apartment.

She didn't look back. She couldn't.

After locking and stacking chairs in front of the door and then pushing the couch in front of it, she fed Muffins and filled his water bowl. On automatic, she started the hot water in the tub. She pulled out yoga pants, a nightshirt, and a sweatshirt and placed them in a nice, folded pile by the tub. She walked to the kitchen and poured a large glass of wine. When the tub was full, she stripped off the memories from the day, and sank into the steaming water.

The hot water soaked away the stress and anxiety. How had she turned from amateur sleuth into a criminal? The day played through her mind on rewind in flashes and bits. She had just as many questions if not more.

Still somewhat in panic mode though, she knew one thing. She had to put Teddy off her trail, and she couldn't do it alone. She needed help.

And she absolutely hated the solution that presented itself. But it was her only option at least that she could see.

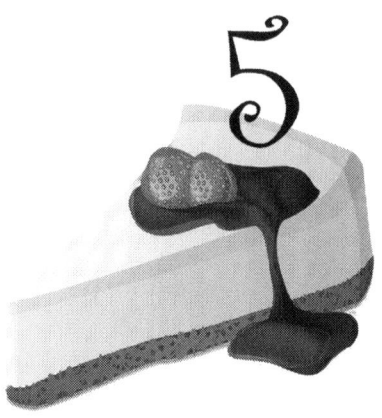

5

EVEN WHEN HOLLY AWOKE in the morning—not the least bit refreshed or rejuvenated—she still hated the only solution that refused to leave her brain. While lying in bed, Holly brainstormed, listing off as many alternative plans.

Admit everything to Trent? Nope.

He was a cop and quite serious about things like dead bodies and potential murder. She didn't want to put him in that position.

Beg for Charlene's help? After all, her friend loved a good mystery.

Scratch that one. Even though Charlene would love the mystery, Holly didn't want to willingly turn any of her friends into criminals. Besides, she was Trent's mother.

Do all the sleuthing herself as in a complete solo job?

Impossible! Even disguised, she'd have a hard time. She had no reason to be in Teddy's house. She needed at least one other person to be a distraction.

Holly groaned. "It's a mystery to me."

Muffins trotted out to the kitchen, probably hungry and in need of a walk. Holly pulled on a sweatshirt and followed him. She really didn't want to think about the body in the freezer at *Just Cheesecake*.

She was pouring the water in the coffeemaker when someone rapped at the door. Startled, her arm moved causing the water to spill on the counter. Was it Trent? How would she explain last night? Like the reason that a murderer who was looking for her was right nearby would go over well. Hardly.

"Holly! It's me!" Millicent said.

Suddenly, she couldn't breathe. What if Teddy had followed her? She glanced at the window, the only possible escape route in her apartment.

"I know you're in there. Hurry up."

"Hold on a sec." Holly moved the couch away from the door. Then, on second thought, in case Teddy showed later, she moved it enough that she could open the door a crack.

She unlocked it. Through the crack, she eyed Millicent holding two cups from *Oodles*. No sight of Teddy lurking in the shadows.

"Paranoid much?"

"You could say that." With another shove, she pushed the furniture a little further. Why put it back into place when she'd stack them back every night from now on?

"Good thing I was blessed with a slender figure." She squeezed through, holding the cups in the air. She narrowed in on the homemade barricade. She handed Holly a cup. "Your favorite. Or what I guessed was your favorite. A mocha latte."

"Thank you." Holly accepted the cup, flooded with thankfulness. The hot specialty drink was exactly what she needed. She unstacked two of the kitchen chairs and they sat.

"How'd it go last night?" Holly asked.

Millicent sniffed as if offended. "He's interested in cheesecake and for some reason only wants yours. This situation is not acceptable and must be corrected."

"And you have a plan?"

"I always have a plan. You need to close the shop for a few days while he's here, so he'll settle for *The Tasty Bite*. Get the focus off you."

"Okay," Holly sipped her coffee. This was perfect. Why hadn't she thought of that? She could slap up an On Vacation sign and hide behind her stack of chairs and her couch. Sneak out at night to walk Muffins.

Millicent frowned. "Gosh, I expected a little bit more of a fight."

"Turning criminal not as exciting as you hoped?"

"Criminal isn't a very nice word. I prefer the term Secret Enforcers of Justice. Hmm." She tapped her chin. "That's not very original. Well, I'll think of something."

"I have a plan," Holly stated. "I need help investigating Teddy's family. I need to prove my father's innocent."

"I don't know about that." Millicent tried to hide her grin. "You Hartfords are a rather sordid bunch. I still don't see what's in it for me. Other than the adventure."

"Fodder for your mystery novels?" Holly sighed. She didn't want it to come to this, but it was all she had left. "I'll close the shop. I'll leave town. Everything you've wanted since the day I moved to Fairview."

Millicent smacked her hand on her knee. "Deal." She paused, a curious expression creeping across the face as if she were cooking something up. "Meet me later in the back room at *The Tasty Bite*. We'll plan everything."

"Deal."

***

Holly stood outside her shop, hair in a bun, wearing a large floppy beach hat. She wasn't taking any chances. The hat might attract attention but it would hide her red hair. If she had to walk outside, she couldn't be a dead giveaway to Teddy. She scribbled On Vacation on a piece of paper and taped it the door of her shop.

"Can I buy you a cup of coffee?"

She stiffened until she recognized Trent's voice. "I'd love to, but I need to get back home."

"Are you going somewhere?" he teased. "The ocean?"

"Maybe. I don't know. I just need a few personal days."

"Is this about Teddy?" He sounded protective, and her heart melted. "Has he given you any trouble?"

"Not exactly." Holly glanced up and down the street. At some point, he'd be back to her shop, and she didn't want to be anywhere near. This made her think of the plan. The only plan, at this point, that could work. Quickly, she pushed it from her mind. One cup of coffee should be safe. "One cup."

They walked to *Oodles* in silence. Inside, Trent approached the coffee bar. Holly pointed to a back corner table. Close to the side exit. Close to a potted fern she could possibly hide behind.

Coffee in-hand, Holly fiddled with the cup. Trent knew her. He'd know she was scheming. If he knew the extent of her plans… He'd throw her in jail. For life.

"How's cop business, lately?" Holly asked, an eye on the door.

"Oh, you know. Chief Hardy. Speeding tickets. False alarms. Nothing too exciting. Which, of course, is good."

"Right. Of course." Her thoughts veered back to her plan, and the fact that, once again, she was paired with Millicent. As much as Holly didn't like her, the girl was smart. Holly barely noticed that a few minutes passed with no conversation. She was consumed with thoughts of bodies and murder.

Possibly her own.

"Hey," Trent said softly.

He reached across and held her hand. Everything in her said to play it cool. His hand felt warm and soft and safe. She liked it. The emotion rushed forward and cracks appeared in her armor.

"Something's wrong. Something is very wrong. I know you." His finger traced the ring he'd bought her for Christmas. "Your past is catching up. You're shutting down the business indefinitely. I want to be there for you."

Blinking back tears, Holly pulled her hand away. "Thank you. You are—more than you know."

"You can talk to me about anything."

"I know."

How would he react to her sins of the past twenty-four hours? How about the body in the freezer? She didn't want to disappoint him, yet she'd love his insight. Unfortunately, that most likely meant playing everything by the book. Regardless of the outcome or jail time.

She wasn't ready to reveal her sins.

6

NORMALLY, HOLLY WOULDN'T CLIMB through the window of the backroom of *The Tasty Bite*.

The same back room where for the past year the murder mystery club had met. And now, she and Millicent would draw the battle plans on how to take down Teddy and his family.

It was also the same backroom where Millicent liked to sneak in some writing time. No distractions. Pastries nearby. And, she was close, in case her papa needed help. Holly admired Millicent's efforts to help her father.

Holly sat in the backroom, floppy hat still hiding her red hair. She didn't think she'd ever take off the hat again. It was after lunch, and while Holly waited for Millicent to appear, she thought back on her conversation with Trent. Her eyes smarted. Darn him. Why did he have to be so thoughtful? So caring? So loyal? For the first time, it hit her. Trent was so much more than her boyfriend. He was her best friend. And she loved him so much it hurt. That was why she'd ended their coffee date early. She couldn't handle being near him. Too long and she'd tell him everything.

When Holly heard humming outside in the hall, she braced herself for the talk with Millicent. With a smile, and a laptop tucked under her arm and a plate of cinnamon pastries in hand, Millicent breezed into the room.

It struck Holly how nice and innocent and charming Millicent appeared when no one was watching.

"Ready?" She placed the laptop and plate on the round table and pulled up a chair. "Don't think I'm going to be the only one putting myself in danger." Millicent shook the pastry at her, cinnamon sugar flying everywhere.

"Definitely not."

"First, take off that ridiculous hat."

Holly felt naked, exposed, without it but pulled it off. Then the door opened and Charlene, Kitty, and Ann walked into the room.

"Oh," Millicent said. "I invited our friends too."

Holly bit back her anger. She didn't want anyone involved who didn't need to be. She forced a smile. "Hi, guys!"

Charlene snorted. "Don't hi, guys, me. Something's going on but Nancy Drew here wouldn't tell us anything."

"Just that the mystery club was meeting," Kitty said, curiosity gleaming in her eyes.

"Tell them everything," Millicent said, her mouth filled with pastry.

Everyone leaned forward, listening. She could've heard a mouse nibbling on a crumb it was so quiet.

"Well, there's been a visitor snooping around town."

"A hottie too!" Millicent said. "He's gorgeous. He's got money. Of course, he's also the bad guy in this story."

Holly watched the dots connect in Charlene's mind.

"So, Theodore decided to visit Fairview?" she said.

"That's his official name." Holly told the group. "I've always called him Teddy. He's the same guy who played a part in the death of my aunt." Holly dealt out the information slowly.

"Yeah, yeah. Childhood friend, whatever. You've probably been in love with him your whole life. Oh, wait, until you stole my boyfriend." Millicent powered up her laptop and clicked a few keys.

"Trent was not your boyfriend." Holly bit her lip. No use dredging up that one. "But I don't want to talk about Trent. He needs to stay ignorant of all this. For now."

"Why don't you tell us what happened," Ann suggested.

Holly filled Kitty and Ann in on the circumstances surrounding her relocation to Fairview, the details of Aunt Lizzie's murder, and she and her family going into hiding. When it came to the part about Sr. Rumford, she stalled.

"Simple," Charlene stated. "Holly lays low until Teddy realizes she isn't in town. I can pose as the owner of *Just Cheesecake*. He'll take one look at me and leave town."

Holly wished it were that easy. "It's a bit more complicated than that. But, it's probably something I should show you, rather than explain."

Everyone looked disappointed.

"Trust me. You'll understand later." She caught Millicent's affirming nod. "This is top secret." Holly shoved the hat back on her head. Halfway out the window, she stopped. "Meet me at *Just Cheesecake* tonight. After hours."

***

IT WAS MINUTES AFTER closing.

Holly waited under a group of trees. She didn't trust that Teddy wouldn't purposefully walk through the town at night. Or break into *Just Cheesecake*.

A cool breeze pushed dark clouds across the moon. Perfect. The darker the better. Once again, Holly wore dark clothing with a hood covering her hair and hiding her face. She was invisible. Living in Fairview. But still, alone. Very alone. Hiding out in her apartment.

Footsteps echoed.

Millicent, also in black, approached *Just Cheesecake*. She searched the parking lot, looking right at Holly but not seeing her. "Figures. She's late."

When Holly was sure Teddy wasn't following Millicent, she stepped from the darkness. "I'm here."

The rest of the club arrived; she unlocked the door and moved inside. Holly walked through the shop. The cakes and bars and cookies crowded behind the glass showcase were looking a bit sad. She passed them and entered the kitchen. She expected some sort of snarky comment about the merchandise, but they seemed to sense her darker mood.

The key to the padlock gripped in her hand, Holly stopped in front of the freezer and faced her friends. "Teddy is not a nice person. His family isn't nice. He almost killed me once, and I'm pretty sure he wouldn't hesitate to try again. There have been a string of robberies in my hometown. In an interview with the town paper, Teddy spewed lies, blaming my family and me on the crime spree. Yesterday, Millicent and I drove back home to check on my parents' property. It had been broken into."

"Isn't that a good thing?" Kitty asked. "Because someone wouldn't rob their own house."

"You'd think so." Holly shrugged, wishing it were that easy. "But what I found was that someone is going to an awful lot of trouble to make my family look guilty. To drive us out of hiding or to increase the manhunt."

Holly unlocked the freezer. Doubt flickered. She was counting on her friends' love of mystery and their friendship, but they should have a choice before they knew everything. She faced them once more. "You can walk away now and be safe. For the first time, we're operating outside the law, even breaking the law. So I understand if you leave."

"Whatever," Charlene muttered. "What kind of friends do you think we are?"

"I'm in," Kitty stated

Ann hesitated, but then said, "Me, too."

Holly opened the freezer.

EVEN HOLLY GASPED. FROST had formed on the hair and mustache, clinging to clothes. He looked...dead. But she hadn't been mentally prepared to see him again.

Her friends fell silent, probably equally as shocked. Probably expecting nothing more than a new cheesecake design. She stammered and stuttered an explanation, but seeing her family friend in such a drastic condition, stole the words from her mouth.

"It's okay. We'll wait. Whenever you're ready," Charlene said.

Holly looked once more and then shut the freezer. "This man is…was my father's lawyer. He was a close family friend and one of the only ones who knew my family and I went into hiding after my aunt was murdered. When I returned to my parents' house earlier today, not only had it been broken into, but…" Holly choked on the words. "But this man had been stabbed and left on our floor to die, and someone was smart enough to frame my father. Or at least tried to by using our kitchen knife."

"No need to explain any more." Charlene faced Holly. "I'm sure you have a plan. Or we'll come up with one. But, I have one question. What will you say if this comes out in the news? If Teddy makes an official accusation?"

"I know!" Millicent cried. "She needs practice." She whipped out her audio recorder and spoke into it. "Sometimes we can live among friends and neighbors while dark secrets and urges hide within. In this case, someone's childhood friend committed murder in cold blood, and left the victim. Alone. He scattered clues to frame a friend and her family."

"What are you doing?" Holly hissed.

"Duh, practicing." Millicent continued, pretending to be Teddy. "It was I, Theodore, who discovered the truth, who followed my gut instinct, and thanks to me, the town will be safe." She clicked Stop, then starting taking pictures.

Holly stepped in front of the freezer. Millicent snapped her picture. The flash blinded Holly, who stumbled back, hit the freezer, then jumped away.

Millicent kept talking in a deep voice. "I knew you'd crack. I knew from the very start you were off. Deep down, you were hiding the killing instinct, the desire for fresh blood—"

Now Holly was annoyed. "Will you quit it? I'm not a vampire and I'm not a murderer."

Millicent eyed the freezer, shuddering, then focused on Holly. "Might as well confess, my dear." She shoved the recorder in Holly's face.

"No." Holly crossed her arms.

"Let me guess." Millicent laughed, a deep chuckle as if she were a man. "Now you're going to try and tell me that I, Theodore, am responsible?"

Holly felt caught off guard. "Well, yes."

Millicent paced. "I can't believe you. I know you'll stoop low to make me look like an idiot. You've been doing it since we were kids. You always were jealous my family had more money." She flipped her blonde hair from her eyes. "Not that

I blame you. I am handsome and sophisticated and the envy of the town. But this?" She pointed to the body. "This is low even for you. You killed someone to frame me."

Holly closed her eyes and breathed deep. She spoke slowly, enunciating every word. "I didn't kill this man."

"Prove it then, Holly. Go ahead. Just try and convince me. Weave your web. Spin your fairytales and convince me."

Holly moved away from the freezer. "This man is my father's lawyer. And—"

"And he's been stealing your money so you killed him."

"No!" Holly cried.

Millicent studied Holly, her gaze darting between the freezer and back to Holly. "This is delicious. So juicy." She rubbed her hands together in glee. She pressed Play again. "Suspect leaves crime scene. Breaks the law. Hides body. We never know the secrets—"

Holly snapped. The present merged with the past. Repressed anger rose to the surface, blinding her. She charged Millicent and knocked her to the floor. The recorder slammed into the ground, skimming the tiles until hitting the wall.

Millicent screamed. "Don't kill me! We're just pretending. Help!"

Holly grabbed Millicent's wrists and pushed them against the floor and then sat on top of her. "I'm not a murderer. I know you hate me. I get that. I don't know why because I never tried to steal anything you have. We've been friends forever. And now this?"

The adrenaline surge dwindled, leaving Holly shaky. She stared down at her captive, expecting to see Teddy, but it was Millicent. Slowly, she stood and let Millicent go. "I-I'm sorry. I got carried away."

Millicent rubbed her wrists. "I'm probably going to bruise." She stared at Holly. "That proves it. You're screwed if they question you."

"You might've gone a little overboard," Charlene said, drily.

Millicent sniffed. Compassion filled her eyes—briefly—before the mask fell. "You seriously broke the law. You could be in major trouble with this whole..." She shook her finger at the freezer.

"I know," Holly whispered. "That's why I need your help. I need all of your help." She turned to Millicent. "You have an in with Teddy. You could possibly help me prove his guilt. Maybe cause a distraction back in my hometown while I do some sleuthing."

The front door rattled.

Millicent peered into the storefront to the door. "Oh, crap." She bit her lip.

"What?"

"It's Teddy."

Holly felt the blood drain from her face and swayed on her feet. Her throat constricted.

Millicent nodded. "I'm sorry."

Charlene motioned to the back door. "Meet him at the front. Tell him what the sign said is true. The owner is on vacation."

Holly jumped in. "Then, use your feminine wiles to convince Teddy to bring you back to his house tomorrow, or soon. I don't know how. Just do it. Then meet us here."

Teddy pounded on the door.

Millicent still looked doubtful.

"That newspaper article was right about the stealing money part, but it wasn't my father. My dad was undercover at the company to find proof that Teddy's father was the one embezzling money. When he got close, they tried to kill him and accidentally the poison went to my aunt." Holly closed her eyes against the tears. From the champagne, she'd swiped for her and Aunt Lizzie to drink. "Teddy's in on it too."

"So you want to send me out to a killer!" Millicent whispered.

"He won't hurt you. Just play along like you have been. Please." Holly didn't know what else to say, but they couldn't hold off Teddy much longer before he called the cops or broke down the door.

Charlene pushed Millicent toward the back door. "It's the least you can do. All the trouble you've caused Holly." She kicked open the door and pushed Millicent out.

When the door closed, Holly sagged against the wall, sliding down until she was sitting on the cold tiles.

Charlene, Kitty, and Ann huddled by the back door, whispering. Minutes later, Kitty and Ann slipped outside. Charlene joined Holly on the floor. "Sorry about that."

"What?"

"Millicent going off her rocker like that. I should've kicked her out before you attacked her."

Holly snorted, and Charlene joined, chuckling.

"I can't say I regret that part." Holly rested her arms on her knees. "But you both got the point across. I'm dreadfully unprepared for any kind of media attack from Teddy."

"From what you've told me though, he doesn't seem the type." Charlene paused, as if treading carefully. "That would be too easy for him. Where's the fun in that?"

"Hmm." Holly trembled. She was right. Teddy was more of a control freak. He proved it by killing a man and setting her dad to look guilty. That scared her more than a media attack. Teddy was unpredictable and dangerous.

"I hate to bring it up but you can't leave the body in the freezer forever."

"I know." Despair gripped hold of her.

"Maybe…you should bring Trent in on this." Charlene held up her hands. "I know. I know. He's a cop. But I'm pretty sure you come first in his life."

The thought of Trent warmed Holly's insides. "I know," she whispered. "He's first in my life, too. It's not that I don't trust him. I don't want to put him in a position where he has to sacrifice upholding the law. That's not fair."

Charlene stifled a yawn. "Point taken."

"Go home. I'll wait for Millicent."

"You sure?" When Holly nodded yes, Charlene added, "About tomorrow. I want to be there with you, but Pierre and I…"

"Don't even think about breaking a date with Pierre for me. Hopefully, we'll be heading to my hometown. There won't be much to do. Enjoy your day."

Charlene left.

Holly sat in the quiet darkness, fighting off fear. It was out of her hands now. All she could do was wait.

***

WHEN THE BACK DOOR opened, the soft click startled Holly awake. Panicked, she scooted across the floor. Was it Teddy?

Millicent strolled through. "Don't be so dramatic, Holly."

"What happened?"

"Oh, not much. Just that I am the master manipulator. What a sucker."

"He's smarter than that. I mean he's really smart. Are you sure he bought it?"

"He wants your cheesecake. His mother heard rumors." Millicent buffed her fingernails against her shirt. "I mentioned I sometimes help you out and that I contacted you earlier. He invited me to meet his mother tomorrow and talk with her about an upcoming event. Looks like we're business partners now, Holly Hart."

Holly sighed, relief flooding her. While Millicent kept Teddy and his family busy, Holly would visit Rumford & Rumford Law and do a little poking around.

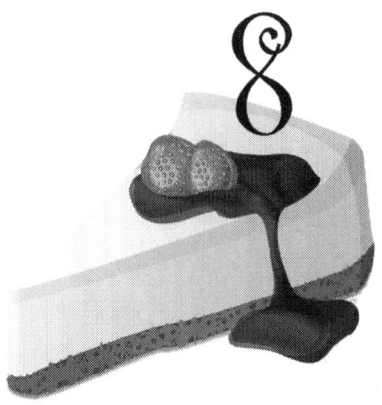

8

THE NEXT MORNING, ONCE again, Holly pushed the couch out of the way and made room between the stack of chairs for Millicent to squeeze through the door.

"Seriously." Millicent huffed, coffee and pastries in-hand. "Someone could force your door open with a few muscle-bound minions."

"Definitely. Most probably." Holly shooed Muffins away from nipping Millicent's ankles. "Sorry. He's a good watchdog. Been more sensitive these past couple days."

"You think that once the bad guys break down your door your little dog will protect you?" Millicent shoved the latte into Holly's hand and dragged a chair over to the table.

"No," Holly corrected Millicent. "It would give me time to get away. Down the fire escape, straight into my car, and then out of Fairview forever.

"About that." Millicent cleared her throat.

"What? Do you want me to sign a contract in blood? I get it. When this is all done, I leave. I disappear. No one will hear from me again. You can finally seduce Trent and solve a murder or two without me."

"No contract." Millicent's voice had softened. She stuck out her hand. "A lady's agreement."

Holly shook. Her heart felt pulled in two different directions. Relief they had a plan to clear her family, but at the same time, great sadness at the thought of following through with her end of the agreement. Leaving Trent and her friends, and this town she called home—forever. "Do you know the details about your outing with Teddy today?"

"Yup." Millicent pulled out a notebook and started scribbling furiously, her pen flying across the page. Line after line of notes.

"And?"

In response, Millicent squealed. "This is incredible. The best thing that has happened."

Holly almost sprayed cold water at her from the kitchen sink. Incredible? The best thing? Maybe Millicent didn't fully realize she was putting herself into harm's way.

"I know what you're thinking. And no, I don't mean the corpse in your freezer or the danger or the fact you broke the law. Though"—she tapped her pencil on the page—"that is a definite bonus."

"Then what do you mean?"

"I mean inspiration. I haven't told anyone, but lately, I've had terrible writer's block. No ideas. My writing has been dog doo-doo. But with last night and this new undercover mission I haven't been able to stop the ideas. If the FBI were to look into the phrases I Googled last night, they'd be knocking on my door."

"Glad I could be of help." Maybe since Millicent was so inspired, Holly would remind her of the danger later. After today was over. "Why don't you fill me in on your plans." While Holly waited for Millicent to finish jotting notes, she finished the blueberry scone.

"There." Millicent slapped the notebook shut. "Sorry. Now, about today. Yes, Teddy and I will be at his parents' house at approximately two o'clock. I will find out what she needs as far as catering, and at the same time, observe for crucial details or clues.

"You won't find anything. They're good."

"We'll just see about that." Millicent stood without eating any of the pastries. She checked the time. "Now, let's go. We have an appointment."

"Huh?"

Millicent giggled. "Trust me, Holly Hartford. I mean Holly Hart. I've got you covered."

After everything they'd been through, Holly didn't trust Millicent. Didn't want to trust Millicent. She was terrified to trust Millicent. Especially when they got into the car and drove out of town and then down a narrow back road that led to a dead end. A ranch sat back in the trees.

"I know Joan from high school. We were friends."

"We shouldn't bring anyone else in on this." Holly braced herself, refusing to leave the car.

"You won't want to miss this. What? Did you think I'd tell her the truth? Come on, you should know me better than that."

Not fully trusting yet, but having no choice, Holly followed Millicent into the dark basement of a house and into the backroom.

"Joan!" Millicent hugged and fake-kissed Joan's cheeks. "You ready to work some magic on my friend here?"

Joan nodded and pointed to a chair. She was petite with short black hair. Nothing about her was cheerful. Her face rested in a permanent frown. She wore no makeup. The only adornment was tiny diamond stud earrings.

Hesitantly, Holly approached and sat. The room had the look and feel of sitting at the hairdressers. Then Holly took in the long mirror, the hair dryers, and scissors, and realized she was in a hair salon.

"I just had my hair cut last week."

Millicent laughed. "Oh, so innocent." She leaned over and caught Holly's eyes in the mirror. "Joan is a master at disguise. She'll fix you up so not even Trent would recognize you. Never mind Teddy or his parents." She stood straight. "Joan understands what it's like to experience a stalker."

Joan nodded but still didn't talk.

"She understands you're trying to get rid of an admirer and you just want to be able to go out in public without being bothered. Joan will fix you up."

Doubtful of Millicent's claims that Joan was the master, Holly was willing to give it a shot.

She listened as Millicent babbled on about high school and boys and prom, and of course, Trent. Holly stopped listening though as she looked in the mirror and watched herself transform.

A fake forehead was attached to a wig of dark blonde dreads that reached her shoulders. Joan colored in darker eyebrows and then attached a fake nose. It looked obvious, but after she sealed it with makeup Holly couldn't tell where the fake met the real. For final touches, she handed Holly a mouthpiece.

"It will be slightly uncomfortable because it's not molded to your mouth, but it should do. Open up." Joan placed the fake teeth in Holly's mouth.

When she looked in the mirror, her jaw dropped. She looked like a completely different person. The buckteeth forced her lip out and then shadowed by the new nose and the new hair, she didn't recognize Holly Hart.

Millicent stood behind her and smiled. "Meet Lacey Stanley."

***

HOLLY GRIPPED THE EDGE of her seat inside of Millicent's car. "No way. I can't do it." Even her voice sounded different with the mouthpiece.

"You have to disguise your voice. Use more of a nasal tone. And you have to do this. Trust me. No one will know it's you. Wouldn't you rather test this out now than have Teddy realize it's you if he sees you on the street?"

Millicent shoved her out the door. "I'll be waiting down the road. Don't want anyone to connect the two of us." The door shut, and Millicent drove away.

It wasn't just her face and hair. Joan had given her blue contacts and a body piece that doubled her cup size. Millicent had added high heels and flashy clothes. Holly's confidence grew. Trent would never recognize her.

She teetered on the heels into the police station. At first, she froze. Chief Hardy with her keen eyes, and Trent, stood by the front desk talking. She hadn't expected to talk with both of them.

Trent smiled, melting Holly's heart. She wanted to blubber and tell him everything. She drew in her emotions. "Oh hello there. My name's Lacey. Lacey Stanley."

"Nice to meet you, Lacey. How can I help you?" Trent asked.

Chief Hardy barely gave her a second look before heading back to her office. Wow. Holly couldn't believe it. The chief wasn't even suspicious.

"Lacey?"

"Oh yes. You see I was walking my dog and a big truck drove by. You know those really big ones that are smelly sometimes."

Trent nodded for her to continue.

"Well, you see. When my little dog heard that loud ruckus, he just plain went and took off on me." Was that country twang Holly added? This was kind of fun. Being someone else. She got caught up in the role. "I chased and chased but with these heels I didn't get very far. And the blisters? Woo-wee. I won't be walking for weeks." She snorted, except it dislodged her teeth. She felt them move, loose in her mouth. Don't panic. Don't panic. Holly covered her mouth.

"What was his name?"

Um, name? Holly wasn't even sure she could talk. "Poochie." It was the first name that popped into her head.

"Poochie?"

Holly nodded. She had to get out of there. "Yes sirree. That's it." Her words came out garbled. She turned to the door and scrambled to adjust the mouthpiece.

"May I have a number to call you in case he turns up?"

With sweat itching her skin under the wig and her body on fire, Holly turned and made up a number. Stumbling over goodbyes, she hobbled down the sidewalk and into Millicent's car.

"Just drive."

"Let's hope you don't screw this up." Millicent snapped her gum, eyes on the road.

It was late morning almost lunch time, and they were on their way for step one of Taking Down Teddy and Avenging Aunt Lizzy. Holly kind of liked the sound of that. For the first time in over a year, that place deep inside that had hidden her grief and sense of revenge, felt alive. She was finally doing something.

"Flirting is a real skill, which clearly you don't have since you came so close to exposing your disguise to Trent."

"I thought I handled it rather well. Considering." Considering her teeth had practically fallen out. "Maybe we should go over the plan."

Millicent huffed. "I get it. You don't need to check on me. I arrive at Theodore's and gracefully enter and win the heart of his parents while observing and looking for clues. I'm pretty good at that if you hadn't realized yet."

"You've never met Teddy's mother. Carolyn is smart." Holly thought back. Carolyn had been sweet and loving their entire childhood, but Holly could see that in comparison to the friendships she had now, it had been somewhat fake.

Millicent's eyes turned into slits. "Bring it on."

They were silent for the remainder of the trip, focusing on their coming challenges. Holly was torn. She had Senior Rumford shoved in a freezer, because she didn't know what else to do without making herself look guilty, and while Millicent chatted with Carolyn, she was on her way to talk to Rumford's son, Chet. As the landscape grew familiar, Holly broke the silence to give directions to Rumford & Rumford Law.

"Do you know what you're doing?" Millicent pulled up along the curb. She sounded rather suspicious, like Holly had no idea what she was doing.

"Yes. I'll get Chet out of the office and find information on Teddy and what the heck is going on in town." Hopefully, her end would go smoothly. No hiccups. "Then I'll meet you at Corner Coffee, three blocks away.

Holly stood on the sidewalk, watching as Millicent drove around the corner toward Teddy's house. He was expecting her at two for tea. With a deep breath, she hobbled on her heels toward the entrance of Rumford & Rumford Law. The whoosh of the air-conditioning greeted her. She rubbed her arms, surveying the room. The office had grown, more desks crammed into the rented space. Impossible to have a private conversation. The atmosphere felt somber, and Holly understood. Senior Rumford was missing, but Lacey Stanley wasn't supposed to know anything about that.

She snapped her gum like Millicent instructed, adding to her persona. "Well, what happened in here? Someone's cat get run over by a truck?" She fake laughed but didn't snort. Her teeth stayed in place.

They looked at her, horror-stricken. Holly cringed. She headed to Chet's desk. "I heard you were the boss and the best."

He didn't look up. "If you could schedule an appointment..."

"No. I need to talk with the boss. Now. I'm leaving town and in desperate need of legal advice." Her words didn't seem to have any effect. "I'll pay you double your hourly rate."

Chet looked up, shrewdly taking in her doctored looks. "Fine. Have a seat then."

"Oh no, Mr. Rumford, Sir." She leaned over, exposing her heaving cleavage. "This is of the utmost secrecy. How about we go for a little walk?"

He eyed her feet. "Are you sure about that?"

She laughed, a large, bellowing noise that would convince anyone. "You're such a cutie." Holly strutted toward the door, hoping Chet would follow.

He did.

On the sidewalk, Holly was distracted for a moment by conflicting emotions. She thought she'd arrive in this burgeoning town and feel homesick for the hustle and bustle. Instead, she found herself missing Fairview. Mostly the people. She wished more than anything Charlene had her back, watching from behind a newspaper on a nearby bench.

"Now. How can I help you?"

She studied him, the dark circles, the aura of sadness. "Is something wrong, Mr. Rumford? If you don't mind me asking, you seem kind of sad."

He sighed. "Can we talk about your matters, please?"

Holly wanted so badly to pull him aside and tell him everything about his dad, about Teddy. For now, she had to keep that secret, but she could reveal herself. She dropped the nasally tone. "Chet, it's me, Holly."

It took a few seconds for her words to sink in as he took in her new appearance, the dreads, the larger nose, and the buckteeth.

"I promise. It's me. Your family has been friends with ours for years. Your dad handled my dad's affairs." Holly knew he believed her, because he stiffened. His fingers curled into fists. Not quite the reaction she was expecting.

He halted and turned his burning gaze on her. "I respect your family, but I suggest you leave before I call Chief Harrison. Only out of respect for the history with your family."

She stumbled over her words. What? Why would he hold such fury toward her? "Chet, what's going on?" She was begging. "This is me, Holly. Holly Hartford?"

"I know exactly who you are."

Ah, the newspaper articles. "Please don't tell me you believe Teddy's lies."

Chet faltered but didn't respond.

"Let me tell you the real truth." It was all or nothing. "My dad was working with Teddy's father to investigate him. Find proof he was stealing money from the company. Not the other way around. Unfortunately, they grew suspicious, and when they tried to get rid of him, they murdered Aunt Lizzie. A complete innocent. We had to go into hiding. In the year I've been gone, Teddy has been poisoning the minds of the town against my parents and me. Oh, I read the articles about me stealing from my neighbors, and it's not true."

Chet pressed his mouth into a firm line.

"I care what the town thinks, especially you." She softened her voice. "But that's not why I'm here."

"What do you want?" he said through his teeth.

Holly motioned to a bench and took a seat. Her feet were killing, blisters forming. She mopped the sweat from her face. Her scalp itched like crazy. She wanted to whip off the disguise. Chet sat next to her, hesitant.

She glanced around. No one seemed suspicious. "I thought I was safe in the small town where I've been living. But Teddy arrived, asking to do business with my cheesecake company. I don't know if he knows I'm the owner or not." Though she was pretty sure, since he'd been digging around. There were plenty of terrific bakeries closer than *Just Cheesecake*. "I need your help." She placed a hand on his arm. "Is there something more to this story?"

He blinked and studied her. "You really don't know?"

What else could there be? Fear rattled her nerves. "No, I don't."

"Just lean back and act normal. They've been watching me in case you or your parents contacted me. I knew but didn't care because of his lies. But I trust you. From the little counter investigating I've done, they claim your father has the money locked away. They want it." He hesitated, then said, "If what you say is true, Teddy's looking for the information your father gathered on his dad."

His words were a challenge. She thought back to her last few days at home with her parents. Her father gathering his thick files.

"You're right. Except I don't know where he put the files." It made sense. Perfect sense. She almost wanted to laugh. "They're scared. That's why they've been working hard to discredit our name. If we bring it to light, he wants our character to be in question."

"Why don't you bring it to light and be done with it?"

"My dad said something about Teddy's father being a small fish. They were after the top of the food chain. So we left." She bit her lip. Now for the favor. "Will you keep your eyes and ears open for anything? Try to talk up my family and counteract the lies?" She didn't want to tell him anything else.

He sucked in a breath. "My dad's missing. Teddy hinted that maybe you had something to do with it."

She squeezed his hand, fighting back the tears and the truth. "I'm so sorry, Chet. I loved your dad." That was all she could manage.

The desire for justice burned hotter. Teddy and his family had to be exposed.

10

"Huge. Ginormous. Tremendous." Millicent's car crept toward eighty.

"Um, Millicent?" Holly pointed to the speedometer.

"Oh, right." Millicent offered a giggle. "Sometimes when I get excited or distracted, I speed up."

"Tell me more about this party."

"Right. Turns out you might be a little paranoid, Holly. Carolyn was an absolute delight. We were like soul mates, both experts in fashion and parties."

"Carolyn's like that. I promise. She's the best at faking it."

"Okay, so she'd heard about *Just Cheesecake* and wants us to cater a big party. I mean huge. Enormous. Fantastic!"

"I get the point." The car surged forward, so she gripped the seat.

"I don't think they know it's you behind the company."

"They do. Gut feeling. Don't forget the frozen goody in my freezer, and the fact they were framing me."

The car suddenly dropped below sixty. "I forgot about that."

It was almost as if Millicent didn't want it to be true. That she could become best friends with Theodore's family and live happily ever after.

"Fine. They might suspect it's you, but I don't think they know for sure. Why else is Theodore returning tomorrow to talk to *Just Cheesecake* about the event?"

Holly gaped. "I thought the plan was that with your charm you'd so convince them of your father's skill that *The Tasty Bite* would do it."

Millicent hesitated, doubt shadowing her face. "I can't put that on my dad. He barely makes it now." Her voice dropped. "His pain is increasing. He might retire."

"Oh. I'm sorry." Not for the first time, Holly wondered if there was some way she could help them. She tucked it away in her mind for later.

She flashed Holly a look. "Of course."

"Regardless of what you've made our healthy and friendly competition out to be, your father and I have nothing but the highest respect for each other. We've both concluded that our businesses are just different enough that we complement each other. It's you that has made it into something negative this past year."

Millicent flashed her a doubtful look and then focused on driving.

"I've got to get this thing off." Holly reached up and stuck her fingers under the wig. Her hair was a sweaty mess.

"Don't." Millicent's hand snaked out and gripped Holly's wrist. "Not yet. I've got a plan."

Terrific. "I'm not sure I want to hear this plan."

"Trust me."

Holly stifled her laughter at the irony of the situation. "Spill it, then."

"Not yet. Just play along. Act in character when we arrive at *The Tasty Bite*.

Doubt and mistrust swelling, Holly followed Millicent into *The Tasty Bite*. She grumbled. "I'm not sure why I have to remain as Lacey. She's proved her purpose. We should probably get cracking on baking the zillion cheesecakes Carolyn wants, because I'm on vacation, remember?"

"Stop mumbling, Holly." At the door to the back room, Millicent adjusted Holly's wig. "Okay, Lacey, do your thing."

Holly walked into the room and had to hide the shock. Everyone was there: Charlene, Kitty, Ann, Trent and Russell, Millicent's on and off boyfriend. They studied her, curious and suspicious. Charlene winked, obviously privy to her new appearance.

"Howdy!" Holly took a seat at the table, the memories of the past year flooding her. All the times the mystery club had made plans in this room.

Millicent didn't waste any time starting. "Thank you for meeting on such short notice. I realize you work hard and it's not quite the end of the day. Trust me when I say we need to work together on this."

"We should probably bring Holly then." Trent gave Millicent the Look.

"If you haven't been by the shop, Holly's on vacation." She pointed to Lacey. "Everyone meet Lacey Stanley. The assistant Holly hired before she left for vacay."

Holly gave a little wave.

"Holly wouldn't do that." Trent sounded firm. "If she needed help, she'd ask my mom and the girls."

Millicent burst out laughing, tears running as she glanced between Holly and Trent. "Fine. Fine. You win."

Holly assumed that meant she wanted Holly to reveal herself.

"Lacey?" Millicent gave the order with just her name.

"Fine." Holly slipped her fingers under the wig and pulled off the hair and fake forehead. She heard murmurs as her red hair was exposed. Then, she peeled away the fake nose and spit out the mouthpiece. Feeling nervous, she flashed a smile. "Hi, everyone. It's me."

Before anyone could talk, Millicent said, "We're geniuses. Not even Trent could spot the difference. Trent was our test yesterday."

"Pfft. I was just about to say something was off about Lacey and the whole situation." Trent eyed Holly, silently questioning.

"This morning, we were back in Holly's hometown doing some investigating work."

Trent perked up as he understood the significance of that. Holly suddenly found the chip in her nail polish extremely interesting.

"As you may or may not know, Holly came to Fairview after escaping scandal in her hometown. Holly and her parents had to go into hiding, and she chose our lovely town. Now, her longtime childhood friend, who's obviously in love with her, is close to discovering the truth. He's been poking around in Fairview with the excuse that he wants *Just Cheesecake* to cater a huge party his parents are throwing. We need to convince him Lacey is the owner of *Just Cheesecake*."

Trent gripped his hat in white fingers and caught Holly's gaze. "This doesn't sound safe at all. I propose Holly stay behind."

Millicent answered. "We know Holly's life is in danger, but—"

"Yes," Holly interrupted. "I'm more than willing to take on the risk." She caught Trent's gaze. "No way am I staying behind and put everyone else in danger. Besides, with all of us working together, how much danger could I be in?"

Trent grunted but didn't argue. He knew when he'd lost.

"Holly and I cannot throw this kind of an event without everyone helping. And I mean everyone. This core group will be the only ones who know the real truth. Theodore's family will believe the owner of *Just Cheesecake* is Lacey. We'll ask anyone who knows Holly to help without questions."

Kitty was the first to speak. "Holly, I'm here for you. Anything you need."

"It's better that none of you know the intimate details," Holly stated. "We don't want Theodore or his family to see anything suspicious."

"What about me?" Trent asked. "I need to know if I'm getting involved in anything illegal or possibly a crime."

"Nothing criminal," Millicent said, then dismissed the idea.

Holly grimaced on the inside. Nothing illegal or possibly a crime? Not really. The body in the freezer was much more complicated than that.

They spent the next hour delegating. Holly said nothing, her thoughts wandering to her parents, to Teddy, to Chet Rumford. Kitty and Ann would be in charge of locating proper uniforms. Millicent, Holly, Charlene, and Pierre would be in charge of the baking.

Millicent cleared her throat and took on a power stance. "We're doing this to throw them off Holly's trail. Convince Theodore that Lacey is the owner of *Just Cheesecake*. Then they'll move on and look in other towns."

It really was quite brilliant. If it worked.

"And, Holly." Millicent steeled her voice. "Tomorrow morning, you're meeting with Theodore to nail down the contract. And...prove to him that Holly doesn't live in Fairview."

Holly gulped. She had to meet with Teddy.

Tomorrow.

11

Holly's hands shook so badly the next morning, she couldn't put the teeth inside her mouth. Instead, she placed them on the counter and sat on the bed. The red digital numbers on the clock on the nightstand were unavoidable.

Forty-five minutes.

That was it. And then, she'd be talking face-to-face with Teddy. Yes, her disguise had fooled Trent and almost everyone in the room the day before. But Teddy?

He was smart and observant. Lawyer smart. Plus, he was suspicious, so it made him more dangerous and her disguise that much more fallible.

"I can do this," Holly whispered over and over to herself.

Muffins sat by her feet, loyal to the end. "I'd love to bring you in on this, but Teddy would recognize you in the time it takes a cheesecake to burn. Not that I've overcooked a cheesecake," she muttered, attempting to laugh at her own joke.

Finally, after a third pep talk that didn't seem to be working, she faced her teeth and the bathroom mirror once again. She put on the cleavage-revealing shirt Millicent picked out with the reasoning that Lacey had to be the opposite of Holly.

Ten minutes later, Holly crossed the street and took down the On Vacation sign from *Just Cheesecake*. She entered her store with an overwhelming sense of nostalgia as if already this business was a lingering memory.

Charlene showed up on time, her unsmiling face at the door as she knocked. Lacey let her inside.

It had been decided, by everyone, that Holly shouldn't face Teddy alone. Charlene had volunteered to act as the assistant, because one, she often was the assistant. And two, they didn't want to put Holly's regular high school assistant, Max, in a dangerous position.

"You sure that silly disguise will fool this guy?" Charlene asked.

"I hope so." She almost added that it had fooled her son.

Charlene put on her apron, then stood at the counter. "Where do you want me?"

Holly studied the shop. What would be the least obvious? "How about you go back and forth between wiping down the tables, working in the back, and then possibly reloading the showcase." Obviously, Charlene couldn't stand in the corner or by Holly's side with a gun hidden in her apron.

"Fine," Charlene grumbled. "Heads up."

For one panicked second—more like several—Holly froze. There he was. Confident and tall. Smart and good looking. Why hadn't she ever liked him? Now the thought made her shudder. Maybe all along she'd sensed he wasn't completely good, that somehow, the kindness he portrayed was an act. That underneath all that... She couldn't finish the thought that someone she'd considered a friend could be a killer.

Charlene hissed from the door to the kitchen. "Get with it!"

The words pierced her awareness as the door opened and Teddy walked through. More like swaggered. Instead of appearing eager to strike a business deal, he stood in the entranceway and observed. He took in the style of tables, the atmosphere she'd painstakingly created, and he took in the smallest details of the pastries behind the showcase.

Teddy knew his childhood friend, Holly Hartford, well. She'd spent years of her life pouring out her hopes and dreams to him. She stifled a gasp as she realized he would recognize her in everything from the floor tiles to the flowers on the tables. Fear rocked her. Why hadn't she thought of that?

Charlene coughed from the kitchen.

The words tripped and stumbled from her mouth. "Well, there, howdy now. What can I do you for?" Did she have to sound like someone who spent their life raising chickens?

His dress shoes tapped the floor. He slowly walked toward the counter, his gaze now focused entirely on her. "Yes." His voice was smooth and powerful, oozing that wealthy air of I-can-do-anything. "I'm looking for the owner of this delightful little cheesecake shop I've heard so much about."

"Oh, really. That's a high compliment coming from an out-of-towner. Thank you very kindly." Her words, her accent, her disguise felt faked and forced.

Surely he would sense the fraud. Wasn't he trained for that? She hid her nerves with a few more phrases about kind strangers and word of mouth and how much she loved cats. That had come in a spur of the moment decision. Holly Hartford, even though she wasn't against cats, was a complete dog person, and Teddy knew that.

He leaned over the counter, his gaze flickering to her chest and then back to her face. What about freckles or moles? Did she have anything like that she wasn't aware of but that he would recognize? There were so many flaws in this plan.

Charlene pushed open the door and breezed through, whistling, with a bounce in her step. She headed to the tables, sprayed, and wiped them down.

He cleared his throat, and her attention snapped back to him. "What were you asking?"

"The owner?" he drawled. "I'd like to meet her and talk business."

"Why yes. Hold on one moment." She rushed to the back, her breathing shallow, and dizziness threatening to overtake her.

Charlene appeared seconds later and yanked her to the back. In a gentle but firm way, she pushed Holly against the freezer. "What is your problem?"

"I can't do this." She thought about Senior Rumford on the floor of her parent's home. She thought about his final breaths. She thought about how it had been pure luck she'd found him when she did. If not, her dad could be in jail right now.

"Yes. You. Can." Charlene pierced her through like her gaze was a medieval sword. "This is what you've been waiting for. Your chance for a little revenge. To play with your enemy when you've got the advantage because you know more than he does.

Holly shook. She didn't want revenge. She wanted to run away.

Charlene let out sigh of frustration. "I hate to do this but think of your aunt. Think of all the reasons this past year why you've been so obsessed with solving murders, with catching the bad guys. You've faced killers, almost been drowned in cement, and seen your boyfriend shot. It's because of the jerk standing at your counter. Now is your time. Go out there and be Lacey. Understand?"

Something flipped inside Holly. Charlene's words struck home. "Oh my gosh, you're right."

"Stop thinking. Just go."

Holly bustled out, adding a bit of swagger to her own walk. "Sorry about that. I hate to keep a customer waiting but some cakes in the oven needed rescuing. Again, what can I do you for?"

Teddy eyed her. "Is the owner available?"

With a gulp of oxygen, realizing it could possibly be one of her last if Teddy recognized her, she said, "You're looking at her, sweetheart. What do you need? A romantic dessert for the girl in your life?" She winked. "Something to sugar her up for after-dinner activities?"

Teddy's face paled like he hoped she wasn't suggesting what he thought she was suggesting because talk like that wasn't proper. Holly Hartford would know that.

"You're the owner?" His tone held disbelief as he regained his composure.

"Sure am. I do everything. I believe in a hands-on business from the top down. I do the cooking, the selling, the washing up." She tapped the counter. "This baby is my pride and joy."

His next words were cold, questions in his eyes. "We're looking for a top-notch caterer for an evening event. Desserts only."

She needed this. "Don't you worry. I have a staff of workers that are nothing but professional. I can cater events and you won't even know we're there. How did you hear about us?"

"Word of mouth."

Ah. He was playing coy. "Well, that's what I love to hear." She yanked out a notebook. "I can do just about anything. Small parties. Large parties. Lavish events the middle class would only dream of attending. Why just the other day I catered an event for Steven Tyler." Okay that might be a tiny lie.

"Are you the only owner? Do you employ any help in the kitchen, say cooking? I see you have a successful business."

That was right. Reel him in. "Of course. I have a slew of people ready to help. You met Millicent yesterday, I believe. Ones who love to cook and want to stay out of the limelight. Others who love to deliver. All sorts." Someone say, like a

Holly Hartford. She could practically see that same thought running through his mind.

His eyebrow lifted like it was attached to a string and someone had given it a good yank.

He proceeded to relay the details of the Saturday evening dinner party that weekend. He knew it was late but he'd been hunting down the perfect caterer. Holly didn't care for the term hunting. She felt like prey. He wanted hundreds of cheesecakes in all varieties, and he'd leave it up to her expertise. Almost as if he didn't trust Millicent would remember what his mother said the day before.

Holly nodded and smiled like everything was completely possible. Never mind the small details like cooking that many desserts and fitting them into her refrigerated truck. She considered the idea that perhaps this was a mistake. It might be better to act incompetent and send Teddy in a different direction.

But, she needed information. She needed to end this. She was tired of being in hiding and lying to her friends.

If not, he might be back another day.

They wrapped up the deal with a contract and a smile. He looked her in the eyes and winked. That was when she had the sinking realization she'd forgotten the contacts that morning. They still sat on her bathroom counter. Had he recognized her? Was he playing with her? Maybe he'd seen right through Lacey Stanley.

"Looking forward to this Saturday. See you then." He waved over his shoulder and walked out the door.

She barely held it together while he climbed in his car and pulled out of the parking lot, then she sagged on the counter and let out a sob.

Charlene's gentle touch landed on her shoulder. "There, there," she cooed. "He was a pretentious jerk. I'm not sure I would've been friends with Holly Hartford, but I am with Holly Hart. So tell me everything."

Holly sobbed. "I forgot the contacts!"

12

SHE KEPT BLUBBERING, THE stress of the last thirty minutes releasing with every tear and hiccup. In between gasps of heaving breaths, she managed to say, "You can't tell Millicent."

Charlene snorted. "Who cares what Millicent thinks? Frankly, I'm not sure why you care so much." She opened the showcase, filled with more than day-old desserts and pulled out a tray. Then she proceeded to munch on a cheesecake bar that was more than a week old.

"I still think you could've proved to this Theodore guy that Lacey is the owner and not Holly without following through with the actual catering gig."

"Probably." Holly shuffled over to one of the tables and sat, her shoulders hunching over. "But I need to dig for information. Maybe find something to hold against him. Or just prove to his mother that Holly has nothing to do with *Just Cheesecake*. If she believes that, then maybe they'll search someplace else." Holly paused, her mind going to the stand-up freezer in the kitchen. It always came back to that.

"True." Charlene brought the platter of sweets with her. "Now, go home. Take a hot bath. Drink a bottle of wine. Do whatever you want. But try to relax and forget about Teddy."

Right. Like that was possible. With the platter in her arms, Charlene shoved her out the door.

***

HOLLY SANK INTO THE steaming hot tub, glass of wine in-hand. She didn't care it was the middle of the afternoon. She didn't care she should be planning with Pierre the baking plans for the next few days. She didn't care about anything at the moment.

She closed her eyes and leaned back. The lavender scent of the bubble bath lured her into a sleepy haze. She sipped the last of the wine. It was only her third glass. Big deal. She deserved it after the last couple days she'd had. She fantasized about the whole thing being over. She'd do the catering event with neither Teddy nor his parents recognizing her, then she'd return to Fairview and pack her belongings. Maybe find her parents. Or possibly take a cruise in the Caribbean and do nothing but play shuffleboard, order too many fruity drinks, and abuse the ice cream bar.

A tear slipped down her cheek. It must be the wine making her emotional. Had to be.

Someone knocked on the door. Couldn't Millicent just leave her alone? Of course, she'd want the complete rundown on the meeting with Teddy. If she'd been smart, Holly would've run to *The Tasty Bite* and told her everything.

She knocked again.

"Hold on!" Holly stepped from the tub, water dripping onto the floor. The room spun around her. Whoa. Too much wine. She dried her hair and wrapped the towel around her body. Muffins followed her down the hall and into the living room. Whenever she was home, he didn't leave her side as if he somehow knew. Maybe he did.

"I'm coming."

She managed to pull a few chairs back, giggling the entire time. She'd gone through the process enough times she had it down pat. "Just let me get this couch out of the way."

For some reason that sounded hysterical. Her sleepy wine had turned into slightly buzzed and giggly wine. She unlocked and opened the door.

"Trent?" she sputtered.

Normally, Holly had good manners. She used restraint, smiled when appropriate, and didn't slam doors in peoples' faces. She gasped and slammed the door. Or she tried to. Trent stuck his foot in the way.

"We need to talk."

Holly took one look at the stack of chairs, the heavy books she'd added to the chairs—just in case—and the couch. She realized water dripped down her back and her towel could slip any second.

She giggled again. "I'm in nothing but a towel."

"I see that."

The whole situation struck her as hilarious. Whatever. She opened the door the full twelve inches. "Sure, come on in."

She settled back and watched in amusement as Trent squeezed his way through the door. He managed inch by inch, but barely. Finally through, he said. "Are you drunk?"

"What?" She patted her chest. "Why would you think a silly like that? I'm a responsible business woman and would never drink too much." She walked to the counter. "Want a glass of wine?" Then she laughed again. Maybe she'd missed her calling as a comedian.

Suddenly he was behind her, his hand on her waist. "I'm not sure you should be drinking any more."

She shook him off. "Thanks for the concern, but really, I'm okay." She filled her glass and one for him. "Here you go."

The fact that water was forming puddles on the floor should've been a signal to go change but for some reason she was enjoying Trent's discomfort, the slight flush to his cheeks as he tried not to be obvious when he snuck glances at her.

"Pull up a chair." Making sure the towel was firmly in place, she dragged one over to the table. This was becoming part of the routine.

"Do I want to ask about the chairs and the books and the couch?" Trent asked.

"I don't know. Do you?" She giggled and took another sip.

"Yes, I do. Why do you have your house fortified like it's Fort Knox?"

"I'm scared of spiders? I don't want any mice or other scary rodents to find their way inside?"

Trent narrowed his eyes, the slight pink in his cheeks growing to a rosy red. "I didn't realize Teddy unnerved you this much." His stern gaze softened and the caring guy she knew returned.

Right in that moment, all she wanted to do was kiss him. Who cared about tomorrow? She was leaving soon anyway, right? If she had to disappear again, she might as well enjoy her last few days. She pulled the chair so she was next to him, their legs touching.

"Possibly." She placed her hand on his leg and left it there. "Nothing I haven't dealt with before." She leaned forward, inches from Trent's face. His lips were so kissable.

"Is there a reason you stopped by? And did you know you have the softest most kissable lips in town? I swear you could win a ribbon at a fair."

"Now I know you've had too much wine."

"Stress can do that to you." She took another sip.

"There are other ways to escape."

"Why, Officer Trinket, are you flirting with me?" She traced her fingers up his arm.

He reached out and touched her soaking wet hair. "Looks like I interrupted something."

"Eh, the water had grown warm anyway."

His hand moved to her cheek, and she sucked in a breath. "Hot baths are highly overrated, especially bathing alone."

"Why Holly Hart, are you flirting with me?" he teased.

"Possibly." She glanced at the chairs. "You might not want to stay. Any second, bad guys could burst in the door."

"I'm a big boy." His fingers moved to her mouth. "And I don't think anyone's bursting through the door anytime soon."

A tear trembled, the stress of this morning still hovering.

He leaned forward and kissed the tears. He whispered, "Anything you want to talk about?"

"Dead bodies?"

"I'm serious. You can talk to me about anything." The depth of caring in his looks, his touch, his eyes were immeasurable.

She pushed his sandy hair from his forehead. "You need a haircut."

"I mean it. Anything," he whispered. "I'm off duty. I'm a friend."

A friend. A part of her knew the wine was affecting her current thought process. He might be off duty, but was a cop ever off duty? To the point he'd ignore things like dead bodies in freezers?

She leaned closer so their mouths were inches apart. The scent of fruity wine and Trent combined was intoxicating. "What if I don't want to talk?"

He didn't answer but his breathing grew shallow and he didn't pull away. She didn't need an invitation but closed the gap and kissed him. Gently. Softly.

More tears trembled. Her emotions got all caught up in her throat. "Just kiss me."

He kissed her.

All she could think about was his touch and the fact that there was too much space between him. As their kiss deepened and Holly couldn't seem to get enough of him, in one swoop, he pulled her onto his lap.

She giggled. "My towel might fall off."

"Just kiss me."

Her heart throbbed, this time with more than just pain, but something else. Did she love him or was it the wine talking?

He pulled away slightly.

She ran her free hand into his hair and pulled him back into a kiss, while her other hand held up her towel, which was loosening.

He placed a hand on her back and pressed her against him. Suddenly she couldn't breathe. When she closed her eyes, the room spun. "Not sure if I'm spinning from the wine or your kissing, Officer Trinket."

"Must be the kissing. And that's Trent. Off duty—remember?"

"Just kiss me and stop blabbering."

Before they entered the time warp of kissing that always happened when she was with this man, she pulled away. If she loved this man, if he were truly her friend, then she could trust him with the truth.

"I have something to show you."

13

HOLLY BLOCKED THE FREEZER, shifting on her feet. Showing Trent the body felt like a great idea in her apartment. But standing in the cold emptiness of her kitchen, buzz wearing off, Holly doubted.

"Maybe this isn't the right timing." She yawned. "Wow, I'm tired. Why don't we head back?" She moved forward but Trent stepped in front of her.

He placed his warm hands on her cheeks then dropped them to her shoulders. "You didn't bring me over here to suddenly realize it's bad timing. In a moment of vulnerability, possibly due to the wine, you decided to trust me with something." He eyed the freezer and then glanced around the kitchen. "I have no idea what this is about. But if you don't tell me, my imagination will kick in, and I'll think the worst. Like you've hidden a body in the freezer."

Holly squeaked. "A body?" She laughed. "Right. Where would I find a body? It's not like they're lying around in the street or in the landscaping outside my apartment. A body." She slapped his shoulder. "Good one."

The awkward prickly silence followed. Okay. Maybe joking and over compensating for Trent guessing the truth wasn't the way to go. She cleared her throat. "It's just a new cheesecake design and—"

She stopped. She stared into Trent's warm but suspicious eyes. He might not like what she was about to reveal, but he could advise her, accept her as a friend, as an off-duty cop. She didn't want to keep secrets from him. He'd find out eventually. She sighed. "Fine."

"Holly?"

She turned, unlocked the padlock, and opened the door. Trent stared, mouth slightly ajar. He obviously wasn't expecting a frozen body.

Her heart sped up to about eighty miles an hour. "You must be wondering how in the world I would end up with a body. Terribly suspicious, I know. Remember when I mentioned in the meeting that Millicent and I visited my hometown? Well, I left one teensy weensy detail out of the story. I—"

"Holly." He grabbed her trembling hands. "You don't have to tell me anything. Leave it to me. I'll dispose of it. We can set you up in a new town." He rambled. That's when she realized something.

She gasped. "You think I did this?" She pointed at Senior Rumford.

"Well, no, of course not." He frowned, hesitating. "Did you?"

"No!"

He sagged, letting out a breath. "Thank God."

"I'd learned of robberies in the neighborhood, so I drove out to check on my parents' house." She shuddered, remembering the scene. "I found him in the great room." She squeezed back the tears. "He died before he could tell me anything."

Refusing to look at the body again, Holly shut and locked the freezer. "He's our family lawyer. Worse, the real killer made it look like my father did it. So, with no choice, one thing led to another..."

"And you felt like you had to hide the body or you probably would look guilty."

"Exactly."

"Except now you have a body to deal with."

"Exactly."

He pulled her into a hug, squeezing her gently. They stood that way for several minutes. Holly soaking in the warmth and safety of his embrace, wishing this whole thing was a bad dream. He let go of her and stepped back.

The hint of a smile passed over Trent's face. "There's only one thing to do."

"I'm doing it. During the party, I'll find evidence against Teddy and clear my name."

"That won't cut it. He's one step ahead of you. The whole town thinks you're guilty. They just need the body to show up. You'll be in prison if you don't hand over the evidence. Or they'll do away with you anyway."

"What do you suggest?" Holly whispered in the dark of the kitchen.

"We go ahead with the party. You pretend to be Lacey and prove Holly Hartford has nothing to do with *Just Cheesecake*..."

"And?" Holly nudged.

"We plant the body on their property."

***

BACK IN HOLLY'S APARTMENT, Trent placed a steaming mug of coffee and two aspirin in front of her. Then he sat across from her. "I'm not saying it will be easy, because it won't be."

"Maybe I should pack up and leave town. Disappear. Be Lacey Stanley for the rest of my life. I can learn to live with an itchy wig and buck teeth."

"As tempting as that might sound, living on the run is harder than it sounds. Nothing is that easy." He held her hand. "And there's no way I'm letting you leave like that."

Holly wanted to tell him the truth. That she might be leaving anyway, but she knew he wouldn't let her. Eventually, Teddy would find her. She had to disappear if for that reason alone.

Holly slumped over at the table and stayed that way for she wasn't sure how long. Then a hand touched her shoulder. "Come on. Let's get you to bed."

He put an arm underneath her and picked her up. She melted into his chest, his warmth. She felt safe and snuggled into him even though she should send him away. He carried her into the bedroom and laid her down.

She looked up at him, sleepy and with the start of a headache. "You're not leaving, are you?"

He hesitated, glancing between the bed and the door.

"Don't worry. I have no great seduction plans. You're safe," she whispered. "I just want to be held."

He turned and left. Holly curled into a ball. She guessed that was a no. Of course, she'd pushed him too far. She couldn't blame him.

Minutes later, he returned.

"You didn't leave!" Holly almost cried.

"I would never leave you." He sounded sad as he handed her a glass of water.

"Thank you." She patted the bed. "Promise, I won't bite."

He lay next to her and gathered her into his arms. A tear slipped down Holly's cheek, but she didn't bother wiping it away. After everything—he was willing to take care of her, to stay with her.

She fought the drowsiness. These were the moments she'd want to take with her. If she were days from disappearing and starting a new life, then she wanted as many of these memories she could pack into the next few days. "There's so much," she murmured.

"Shh." He kissed the back of her head. "Don't worry about it."

"I do worry. I hurt you and I don't like to hurt the people I love. I love this town and everyone in it. I love my friends..." What was she talking about? She couldn't remember. All she could think about was Trent snuggled up behind her. Right now, he was here. "Please, don't leave." She could feel sleep pulling at her. "I love you."

In the morning, everything would be clear. She'd straighten everything out. In the morning...

12

WHEN HOLLY WOKE, HER head throbbed. What a night. What a day yesterday. Her first thoughts went to Teddy, and that somehow, miraculously, she'd managed to convince him she was Lacey Stanley. They were catering an event to hide the body, which wasn't really a crime because Teddy's family had to be behind it. Holly had a feeling she was seeing just the fringes of the crime that ran through his family.

Something rustled in the bed behind her.

She froze, fear spiking. Then the memories rushed through. The wine, the kissing—oh my God, the kissing—and Trent slept over.

"You awake?" he asked softly.

She tried to remember all the details from last night but they were foggy. She would never again drink that much wine. He was in bed with her.

Her last words before dropping off swam in her mind. I love you. Hopefully, he hadn't heard them. Hopefully, it was her imagination and she'd hadn't said them. Hopefully, her bedroom floor would open and swallow her, transporting her to another time.

"And, I don't plan on going anywhere either."

She rolled over, taking a breath at the sight of him. She could get used to this way too easily. How could she leave in a few days—forever—when she felt like this? Everything in her beat in time with him. Everything in her wanted everything in him. Long term. Serious. Forever. She didn't regret saying those words. I love you. Even if, when this were over, she'd be gone.

He pushed her hair behind her ears. "I don't like this Teddy guy. I don't like that he's sniffing around in town.

Obviously, you're scared of him or you wouldn't have your living room stacked against the door."

What could she say? It was true. "It's just a precaution."

"And it's just a precaution why I'll be staying with you for the next few days until this is over."

Right then, not worried about morning breath, she leaned over, and kissed his mouth, then pulled away.

"Oh, no you don't." He reached around and pulled her to him again, crushing his lips against her. No time warps this time. He broke the kiss way too early, leaving her a bit stunned and dizzy. "I'll be back tonight with my bags. I hope you don't mind. I don't mean to intrude..."

"I want you here." It was all she needed to say.

She jumped in the shower and dressed. They ate breakfast together, not saying much. She had to shore up for a day with Millicent. At least, she'd be baking.

After Trent had left, Holly didn't rush to *The Tasty Bite*. She lingered over a third mug of coffee.

Someone knocked on the door. "Holly, it's me! Hurry up and move your Great Wall of Furniture."

Holly pushed and shoved until Millicent could fit. "Come in."

"About time." Millicent flounced into the room, her keen eyes taking in everything. Holly hoped Trent hadn't left any traces of his presence. Millicent whipped out her notebook. Pen at the ready, poised to write. "We have a lot to talk about."

"Why don't we wait until we're together?" Holly suggested.

"Hey, that's fine. I'll leave it up to you, then. It's not like we only have a few days before the big event and we've done nothing. Never mind the fact that you—"

"Fine. You're right." Holly tried to relax. "What do we need to talk about?"

"Right. How'd it go with Theodore?"

"It's a done deal. We're set to go."

"Good." She wrote in the notebook. "I thought we should plan out the schedule for the next few days. We'll be baking up a storm." She tapped the paper then proceeded to list out all the desserts, the ingredients, and the baking schedule. Holly let her.

When Millicent finished, Holly knew what was coming next. Maybe if she brought it up first. "I have a plan."

"About the body?"

"Maybe. I was talking with Trent—"

"What?" Millicent exploded. "Why were you talking with him? Did you tell him everything? You did, didn't you? You told him about the body."

Anger, hot and furious, rippled through Holly. "You expected me to completely lie to him? If that's what you think relationships are all about, then no wonder…"

"No wonder, what?" Millicent's voice sounded small and hurt.

"Nothing." As much as Holly wanted to list Millicent's dysfunctional views on relationships, she held back. She gritted her teeth, then forced herself to relax. "I talked with Trent because I couldn't keep him in the dark any longer. So I showed him the…unfortunate situation. He had a brilliant plan. That we should plant my dear family friend at Teddy's house and then make an anonymous call. Then Teddy and his family will appear guilty, and we'll be off the hook." Talking through the plan made Holly feel better.

It would all work out. Just as planned.

"We'll be off the hook?" Millicent pointed out. "Don't you mean you'll be off the hook? I'm not the one who killed someone and hid the body."

"I didn't kill anyone." Holly wiped the spit from her mouth.

"Right. You were set up." Millicent sighed. "Regardless, that's a horrible plan, but I suppose you two are already set on it." She pouted. "You could've called me over, you know. My brilliance could've helped."

"It happened so fast or I would've."

"That is risky and hard. You'll need my insight to pull it off."

"Of course," Holly gushed. "That's why I'm telling you, your highness." Did she really just say that? She meant to think it. One look at Millicent's disgusted expression told her she'd said it out loud.

Millicent closed her notebook and stood. "Well, I'll see you over at *The Tasty Bite*." About to slip out the door, she said, "Considering your life is at stake, you should probably take this more seriously. You can't rely on me for everything."

Then she left.

15

THEY MET AT *THE TASTY BITE*.

Holly wore her floppy hat and hid her hair. Slightly paranoid. She hated leaving Muffins in the apartment, but if Teddy or his men were around, her dog would be a dead giveaway.

"You really think Teddy cares about you this much?" Millicent asked rather flippantly. She was dressed in pink with an apron around her neck and covering her clothes.

Holly remembered what Chet Rumford had shared: that Teddy and his parents thought she knew where her dad hid the incriminating evidence against their family. "I don't think he cares about me. He cares about himself. About his future."

Charlene flashed her commanding look at Millicent. "We're going to assume the worst and take precautions."

That seemed to keep Millicent in check as they got to work mixing the cheesecake batter in large batches. While they mixed and baked, they also planned. Holly told them that in the basement attached to the kitchen, there was a large freezer. At least there was during the years they were friends. They didn't plan much while Pierre was there, but by afternoon, when the pain grew to be too much, he stepped out. They used that time to talk.

It was during this time Holly understood Millicent's motivations a little better. If her father was in that much pain, there was no way the bakery could continue too far into the future. From the looks of it, Millicent had been picking up the slack while also working at the daily paper and writing her novel. For the first time, even though Millicent had been horrid by blackmailing her, Holly felt sympathy.

Every night, she returned home, exhausted physically and mentally. Every night, Trent had dinner made. After dinner, they sat on the couch until one of them made the first move. The rest of the evening was spent making out. Like the gentleman he was, every night, he lay on top of the covers and held her until she fell asleep.

The day before the big event, Holly arrived at *The Tasty Bite*.

Millicent studied her. "Why are you so happy?"

Holly relaxed, letting the smile fade. She was happy because she was with Trent. She was ignoring what was coming the next day, ignoring that she'd soon move away, and focusing on each day and the memories she would treasure. "I'm not. I smile when I'm nervous."

Millicent laughed. "I hate when that happens." Then she fell silent.

They worked hard, putting the finishing touches on all the cakes and packing them. Millicent, Charlene, and Holly would meet, cloaked by the darkness the next morning, to load the body into the truck, followed by the cheesecakes.

That afternoon, they met with the team. Holly's heart welled with thanksgiving as everyone showed to help. Anyone who meant anything was there. She let Millicent take over and give the instructions. She watched her friends as they received the orders. She also couldn't take her eyes off Trent.

Tonight was her last night spending time with him. She wanted to make the evening special.

When he walked through the door, she had it all ready. An old blanket was spread across the floor with a picnic.

"What's this?" he asked. "And I was all set to cook dinner."

"You've done enough. Staying here. On the watch. And cooking every night. It's my turn." She fell silent. So much she wanted to say but so much she couldn't.

She poured the wine—determined to have only one glass tonight—and set out the dinner of fried chicken, fresh veggies, and grapes on paper plates. "It's not much."

"It's enough." He sat beside her.

What could she possibly say to show everything she was feeling and thinking? He knew there was more going on, yet he didn't press the issue. Of course, he didn't know what.

Slowly over the week, he'd convinced her to move the couch back and then the chairs and leave the door unlocked until they went to bed. Slowly, the fear of this event, the fear of Teddy and his family, faded. But tonight was different. Tonight was a mix of sadness and anxiety and love. Tonight was about the hope of possibly gaining back her freedom but losing everything.

"That was delicious," he said, offering her a hesitant smile.

"Thank you." They didn't talk much, comfortable in the silence and with each other. There was too much to think about, too much that couldn't be said until it was all over. Holly didn't want her last night though to be about nothing. She also didn't want it to be about kissing, so she started off by asking him about his childhood. Then, for the next hour or so, they exchanged stories, transforming moments in their lives.

He pulled her into his arms and they stayed that way for a while. He promised in soft murmurs and whispers that everything would work out.

There was a quick knock on the door before it opened.

Holly jerked away from Trent, unsure who would open the door if it weren't Teddy. She gripped Trent's arm.

Millicent slipped into the room with a plate of cookies. Her face went from smiles to shock to embarrassment to dismay. She took in the arrangement, the romantic picnic, the wine, and the grapes they had been feeding each other while talking. How close they still sat on the blanket.

Holly could almost see the wheels turning in Millicent's mind, putting the pieces together. The morning Holly had arrived, glowing from her time with Trent even in the midst of their most dangerous, personal case yet. Not that it was a crime to participate in a blanket picnic with your boyfriend, but Millicent's face said it all.

She still—in a teenage infatuation sort of way—loved Trent.

In a way, Holly felt aghast at the past several days too. She'd done everything possible to forget about catering and the body, all they had to do at the party and how hard it would be to pull it off. Had she given her best effort? Probably not. But a part of her was exhausted from fighting it. Whatever would happen would happen. Right?

Millicent giggled, blushing. "Silly me. I thought you might be preparing for tomorrow so I brought over some dessert, and I could give you a pep talk. Be your cheerleader…"

When Trent tensed, Holly gripped his arm. For the first time, Holly believed Millicent's intentions. She was there to help and encourage. Should she ask her to stay? Smooth over the awkwardness?

Millicent's face was pale. Even though she was putting on a good show, Holly sensed that underneath the charade, Millicent was hurting. Not because of their so-called friendship, but because she truly loved Trent—or thought she did.

Finally, Holly sputtered out the invitation. "Um, come on in. Join us. That was exactly what we were doing. Preparing."

Trent raised an eyebrow.

Holly squeezed his hand. Who said enjoying a moment of bonding with your boyfriend wasn't preparing?

"No, really. I wouldn't want to interrupt you two love birds." Millicent took a step back. Finally, she straightened as if remembering who she was and that she wasn't the kind of person to admit defeat. Or show when she was hurting. When she spoke, her words came out a whisper, "I don't care what you do. If this was happening to me and the defining moment of my life was the next morning, the most dangerous mission ever where my reputation and freedom was at stake, I'd be in bed. Or soaking in a bath. Or something." She stumbled the last few steps to the doorway. "And I'd do it alone!"

"Now wait one second here." Trent stiffened.

Holly laid her hand on his arm, signaling—or hoping he'd get the message—to say nothing. That nothing would help right now.

Millicent's eyes opened wide then narrowed in understanding. Like she knew Holly hadn't told Trent she was leaving town yet. She backed away, a smile sliding onto her face that Holly didn't trust. "Um, see you tomorrow morning."

Then Millicent was gone.

The romantic, cozy atmosphere was sapped from the room. Holly felt worse than ever. The reality she'd been ignoring rose between them. It was time to confess. "Not sure of the outcome of our plan. As good a plan as it is." She didn't want to offend Trent. "Not sure how many people are working for Teddy, even if he does go to jail. Not sure exactly how far his reach expands…"

There was a moment of silence. Holly couldn't think of one random fact or useless piece of trivia to fill it.

"You're leaving town. Aren't you?" Trent asked, the hurt layered between the words.

"Possibly." She sagged. She'd been pretending the past few days, living in a fantasy. "But, only—"

"Nope. Don't say a thing." A mask fell over his face. His cop expression. Revealing nothing. "You don't need to explain yourself. But Millicent was right about one thing.

You need your rest. A full night's sleep. Tomorrow will be tough."

He unfolded a blanket from the couch. "I'll sleep out here tonight. You don't need me taking up your thinking space."

"Thank you," she whispered, before heading back to her room. There was so much more to say, but not the right time to say it. Trent was hurt. Holly didn't know if she'd made the right decision or not.

Later in bed, she stared at the ceiling. She didn't want to leave Fairview, but even if the mission tomorrow were a success—would Teddy truly leave her alone? What if planting the body failed? Wasn't it just a matter of time before he picked up the search again? Or he got out on bail and came after her? Or hired someone to do the dirty work? Trent was already putting his career and reputation at risk for her. Her friends, too. But how could she explain that?

It all depended on what happened the next day.

16

HOLLY SLEPT ON AND off. She woke seconds before her watch alarm went off and silenced it. She slipped out of bed and into dark clothing. They'd decided to wear traditional black, and add white aprons at the last second. Classy.

Trent still slept on the couch, so Holly didn't wake him. If she were to be honest, she was avoiding awkward conversation. What if he didn't want to help?

With a last glance at him, she left. She had the rest of her life to be sad and mourn her relationship with Trent. Today was about making sure she had a future that wasn't spent in a maximum protection prison for women. Or worse, six feet under.

She crossed the street to find she was early. She went into the shop through the back door and went straight to the freezer. Somehow, the body inside represented everything she'd been avoiding. She unlocked the padlock and opened it.

Senior Rumford.

Tears sprang to her eyes. She fell to her knees, weeping. "I'm so sorry." She grieved for his son, Chet, who would soon learn why his father had been missing. She wished she could take it all back. She wished she'd arrived at the scene early enough to bring him to the hospital even if it meant she'd be the first one accused. She wished she'd gone right to the police, but at the time, in the moment, this had seemed like her only course of action.

Holly sensed Charlene's presence before she spoke.

"You know this isn't your fault." Charlene approached.

"But it is." Guilt wracked her body and mind. "If it wasn't for my family, he'd still be alive."

"From what you've told me, he knew what he was getting into. He knew your father was investigating this family, and he stayed on the case." She paused, then said,

"Could you have handled things differently this week? Maybe."

Another voice entered the conversation. "Talking about me?"

Holly tensed. Millicent. Would she still go through with today? Every person was needed. The plan was simple. Plant the body. Catch the bad guys.

"I know you like to believe you're the center of conversation, you're not." Charlene straightened.

For a brief second, hurt and regret flickered, before the mask fell. Millicent was once again the sarcastic, demeaning witch she'd always been. "Let's get going. I'm missing my beauty sleep for this."

They worked and moved quietly. It was hard placing a body into the bag Charlene had acquired, but they managed—only dropping him a few times. Holly had to excuse herself to throw up.

"Just remember," Charlene said. "He'll get his justice."

With grim expressions, they carried him into the back parking lot where the refrigerated truck was waiting. They put the bag down, and Holly pushed open the back door.

A bright light flashed in their eyes. Holly felt like your typical robber, caught, blinded by truth and justice. The light focused on the bag, which unfortunately looked exactly like it might be hiding a body.

"Starting without me?" Trent kept the light trained on the ground so they could see him. His face fell into shadows and she couldn't read his expression.

The heat of guilt rushed through Holly. She should have wakened him and told him she was leaving early. But, it was easier when he wasn't there. "I thought you might want the extra sleep."

Completely lame excuse.

"Let's finish the job," he said.

Holly didn't blame him for feeling hurt and betrayed, because she'd kept what would be a major decision from him. Between any of the kisses or romantic dinners or early-morning moments she could've told the truth.

If only Millicent…

No. Holly shook that thought away. She couldn't blame Millicent for this. Time to move ahead with the plan and focus on clearing her family's name. Millicent wasn't the guilty party here. Teddy and his family had to be the focus.

Charlene stood, gaping at Millicent. With narrowed eyes, she then studied Holly and Trent. She bit her lip as if holding back her thoughts. Of course. Holly's dearest friend always sensed when something was wrong.

Eager to divert Charlene's attention and ease the rising tension, Holly walked to the body bag. "Dawn is coming, and we have to have the truck ready before the town wakes.

In silence, the nippy air making Holly shiver, she worked with Millicent, Charlene, and Trent to load the body and then start on the cheesecakes and desserts. They were halfway through, when Charlene stopped. Holly noted the way she trembled, her cheeks flushed.

"Charlene?" She spoke softly.

Millicent walked out of *Just Cheesecake*, carrying only two boxes. When she neared the truck, Charlene attacked, plowing into Millicent and slamming her against the truck. The cakes went everywhere.

"What was that for?" Millicent cried.

Holly moved to step in between them, but Charlene stopped her with her words. "What was that for—seriously?"

Millicent bit her lip.

Charlene slammed her against the truck again. "I've never wanted to kill someone before now. Ever! You've been sabotaging my son's relationship from the minute he met Holly."

"Mom—"

"Not now Trent." She glanced at him then back at Millicent. "I don't know what. But you've done something else. I can feel it in the air."

"Well. It's not... I mean..."

Charlene loosened her grip, disgusted. "I don't want to hear your pitiful excuses. Ever. Again. You will follow through with our plan for today. You will keep Teddy distracted just as planned. If you so much as move to betray Holly again—"

"You'll what?" Millicent spit out. "I'm not the one who's been lying for months. I'm not the one who's leading your son into compromising his career. Did you ever think about that? Huh?" Millicent shoved Charlene away. "Your little golden girl here turned out to be like the rest of us. Her golden shine was just that: a gilded cover that fooled everyone. And I'm tired of everyone thinking she's God's gift to Fairview, dropped from the heavens with miracle cheesecakes that can stop everything from constipation to love problems."

Charlene stayed calm. "I'm going to say this once. Holly has more guts, more kindness, and more goodness than you'll ever have."

"Whatever. I see she still has you under her spell."

"I know everything," Charlene stated. "I've known everything from early on. I knew Holly was running from bad guys and needed to keep her past a secret. I knew you were blackmailing her out of jealousy and spite and this fairytale notion that you and Trent are soul mates."

Millicent gasped and wiped her eyes. "I get it, Charlene. No need to say anything else." She bent to pick up the dropped boxes.

Normally, Holly would've felt a surge of satisfaction that Millicent had finally been put in her place. Strangely, she felt nothing but exhaustion from dealing with her. "It's okay, Charlene. Millicent hasn't done anything this time."

"It doesn't matter about this time. It's the actions and snippy comments she's made over the past year." Charlene focused on Holly. "She might not have done anything directly to cause the tension I sense, but she's got something to do with it. Guaranteed." She turned to Millicent. "Are you going to follow through today?"

"What if I don't?" Millicent asked flippantly.

"You don't want to find out."

They stared, the tension building. Holly shifted back and forth as a rosy dawn tinged the air. They needed to finish. "Maybe we should finish?" she squeaked.

Charlene stood back, and they finished loading the truck in record time. "We'll meet here as scheduled."

17

THE REST OF THE day passed too slow and too fast at the same time. Holly stood, dressed as Lacey Stanley, in front of her freezer, her arms lifted in a desperate attempt to dry the building sweat. She couldn't wait any longer. With a deep breath and quick mental cheering up, she grabbed her purse.

At the door, Muffins nipped her ankles. She bent, and of course, it was her dog that brought on the tears. She pulled him into her arms. "Oh, Muffins. You know I'd bring you with me, but I can't. It's too dangerous." Then she thought about it. Why not bring him? Wasn't he meant to be a watchdog and alert her to danger? She stared him in the eyes. "Promise to stay in my purse? And be quiet?"

He turned the best pair of puppy-dog eyes on her she'd ever seen.

"I'll take that as a yes." She rushed back to her room and grabbed the larger purse. She placed Muffins inside. "Now, let's go."

As planned, Trent drove the truck, along with Russell and Max. Kitty drove Lindsey, Millicent, and Ann to Teddy's house. Charlene rode with Holly—or Lacey. It was a quiet ride. Holly gripped the wheel tighter than needed and reviewed the plan.

Millicent was gorgeous as usual. Dressed in her best, makeup on, and perfume light and seductive. She would distract Teddy with her smile and some champagne laced with a depressant, while Charlene and Holly brought in the body and planted it in the freezer.

Holly wished for a manual on how to do this sort of thing, a formula that would guarantee success.

Way too soon, they pulled into the back of the house, nearest the kitchen entrance. Charlene finally spoke. "Just focus on this evening. Don't worry about Millicent or Trent. Everything will work out. Okay?"

"Okay." Holly blinked back tears.

She still felt vulnerable even dressed and acting as Lacey. She clomped into the kitchen, the very image of an obnoxious redneck that would drive Teddy's mother crazy. Caroline stood in the kitchen as Holly expected.

"You must be Caroline. My what an amazing house you have. I could fit five of mine inside yours." Then she laughed, careful not to snort and mess up her fake teeth.

"Why yes." Caroline smiled while failing to hide her disdain. "Nice to meet you." She offered a limp handshake. "I've heard marvelous things about your cheesecake. I simply had to have them at our party. I hope and expect the service lives up to the cheesecake."

"Oh, it will, Ma'am. It will."

"Good. Then I'll leave you to your work."

When Carolyn exited the kitchen, Holly sagged, trembling and weak. Being in this house, in this kitchen, brought on an onslaught of memories. How had she not known all those years? Teddy had been her best friend, but somewhere along the road, he'd fallen under the influence of his parents. He went one way, and Holly went another.

Charlene appeared at her side. "You can do this. You need to inspect the house and act like you're in charge."

"Right," Holly mumbled. Right! She shook off the overwhelming sadness and gripped her purse. "Let's go."

They walked through the downstairs. Carolyn had gone all out with flowers and elegantly placed decorations, lit candles, potted plants, and pictures of her family. Tall circular tables had been brought in for guests to stand around and chat while they sipped and snacked. A bartender stood behind a bar, waiting to serve drinks. Millicent stood with Teddy, giggling and distracting like planned.

Teddy cast Holly a look, so she averted her eyes and barked out a command, clomping through the rest of the room.

Her friends, dressed as servants, brought in the food, and then when guests started to arrive, they moved through the crowds with trays of desserts.

It was like a punch in the gut to see Trent. He was her emotional safety net, a confidence booster. He could've been rounding up a force to interrupt the party and arrest her for murder. Instead, he was here, helping.

Charlene came alongside. "Ready?"

"No."

Hopefully, the drugs were coursing through Teddy's veins. Just enough to lower his guard.

Hopefully, the party guests were getting their fill of cheesecake and drinks.

Hopefully, Carolyn would be so involved in hosting that she wouldn't notice two of the caterers slipping out the back door.

The spring evening air rushed across her skin, sending an outbreak of goose bumps. Holly rubbed some heat into her arms. This evening reminded her of a similar evening almost a year ago, when she discovered her Aunt Lizzie. Her parents were the ones having the party. She and Teddy technically were still friends. He'd even suggested a long-term relationship leading to marriage.

Charlene and Holly worked side by side. Quiet. Tense.

In the back of the truck lay the body bag. A lumpy shape that caused Holly to shudder. "I hate that Chet is going to find out like this. I hate that we're using Senior Rumford in this way. It feels wrong."

"Sometimes the right thing feels wrong...until it's right. I didn't know the man, but if it were me, I'd like to know my death brought down the real bad guys. Even if it meant someone I trusted carted me around in a bag." Charlene climbed onto the truck. "Let's do this."

Holly allowed her friend's words to temporarily calm the rising guilt. It was harder than they expected—without the third person—to heave the body up onto their shoulders.

"I can't do it," Holly whispered. "I can't do this if we're going to keep dropping him." Her fake size DD cups and sweating scalp were also not helping.

"What do you want to do—bring Russell in on this?"

Holly peeked out the van and studied the lawn and the back of the house. "We'll drive the truck to the backdoor."

Charlene raised an eyebrow. "Over the landscaping and the flower garden?"

"Yup." Holly stepped into the driver's seat and placed her purse on the front seat. She gave Muffins a quick smile and pat on the head. "That's right. You're being such a good doggie."

With a quick prayer, hoping no one, particularly Carolyn, would notice the truck barreling through and trampling her prized flowers. It brought Holly a smidgeon of satisfaction that disappeared when she delayed once more and ran inside to grab a rolling trolley cart.

In the kitchen as she pushed the cart, she ran into Carolyn. Tiny beads of sweat rolled down the back of Holly's neck.

"Is something wrong?" Carolyn asked.

"Not at all." Holly offered a smile. "Just bringing in some more of my dee-licious cakes."

"Yes," Carolyn said drily, studying her. "They do seem to be a hit. My intuition is never wrong." She waved a hand. "Carry on." She made her way back to the party.

What was it about Teddy's mother that drained Holly of all energy? With weak knees, Holly pushed the cart back outside. Together, Holly and Charlene dragged Rumford to the edge of the truck and pushed him onto the cart.

They strolled into the kitchen and then thankfully rode the elevator to the basement. Holly had happy memories of she and Teddy taking it down to sneak more desserts during dinner parties.

It took thirty minutes for Holly and Charlene to empty the freezer and hide the contents in a darkened corner of the basement, and then transfer Rumford into the now empty space. They closed the freezer.

Holly laid her overheated body against the freezer. She fought back the tears.

"You going to make it?" Charlene asked.

"Eventually." She refused to think about Trent.

"I'll get the truck off their lawn before the witch has a conniption and turns everyone into stone with one evil glare. Then I'll join the party."

"Thanks." Holly pulled Charlene into an awkward hug. "Thanks for everything."

"Oh, don't go getting all mushy on me now." But before she walked away, Holly noticed the glint in her eyes.

Alone, Holly placed her hand over the freezer. "Sorry, old friend. Promise. I'll make things right."

The door opened at the top of the stairs. Millicent's high-pitched voice carried down. "Theodore, what's wrong?" She giggled. "I suggested a quiet place where we could get to know each other better, but I didn't mean the basement."

18

HOLLY RACED INSIDE THE elevator and slid the door closed, leaving a crack. Teddy half stumbled down the last few steps. At the bottom, his gaze darted around the basement as if looking for something...or someone.

Millicent walked up behind him. She tiptoed her fingers up his back to his neck. Then, in typical Millicent fashion, she placed kisses on his exposed skin. "But the basement will do."

When finding the basement empty, Teddy turned and responded to Millicent, but the red flags were obvious as they flirted. He embraced Millicent and drew her into a long kiss. Flustered, she broke it off.

"What's wrong babe? What happened to me and you having quiet time?" His voice sounded strange, alarming.

"I...I just didn't expect to move so fast."

"Really?" he sneered. "You've been plastering me with drinks all night while not drinking many yourself. Almost as if hiding your real intentions."

Millicent did her best to cover her nervous smile. "I didn't want to get drunk on the job and forget anything. How about we move upstairs?"

"How about you kiss me." He yanked her to him and kissed her hard. His hands went to her waist and in one move he placed her on top of the freezer.

As he kissed her neck, he spoke, soft and menacing. Just loud enough Holly could hear.

"You seem to be a smart girl. Sophisticated. Willing to get ahead. I don't know why you got stuck in a town like Fairview, but you deserve better."

For the first time Holly could remember, Millicent didn't say anything. Holly felt bad. When Millicent agreed to take on the task of distracting Teddy, no one expected that to be the dangerous job. How could Holly forget Teddy was smart? Too smart. Even if Millicent wasn't her friend, Holly couldn't leave her.

Teddy slipped something out of the back of his pants. Something black and hard.

A gun! Holly stifled a gasp.

Millicent turned rigid but her face remained expressionless. Holly could only imagine the fear coursing through her body.

He traced the gun along the side of Millicent's cheek. "How about we cut the flirting and you tell me what I want to know. You're beautiful, but I'm taken. Sorry, babe."

"That's okay." Her words came out shaky.

"I know you think you're smart, but I knew from the start that this stupid bakery business had to be Holly's idea. You see, we were best friends. She spilled all her secrets to me, and I never forget them. When she so rudely left town, I knew exactly what she'd do." He chuckled. "Of course, her full name on the business application helped too."

Holly curled her fists so her nails dug into the palms of her hands. Of course. How could she underestimate Teddy? How could she be so stupid? She thought she'd taken precautions.

"F-Fairview is a wonderful town."

"Shut up." He reached up into her short hair and pulled her head back. "I'll let you know when it's your turn to speak."

She kicked him between the legs, but he was too fast. He pressed against her, trapping her legs between his body and the freezer. Then he yanked harder on her hair. "Who's in charge here?"

When she hesitated, he yanked again.

"Y-you are."

"That's good," he purred.

Holly was disgusted. She didn't recognize her childhood friend in the least. His parents had corrupted his good nature, turning him into this beast.

He continued. "How about you tell me where to find Holly, and I'll think about letting you live."

"I don't know who you're talking about."

Holly couldn't take it anymore. This wasn't what Millicent had signed up for, but here she was, covering for Holly. If Millicent truly hated her, she would've given her up at the first sign of trouble. In the span of two seconds, she forgave Millicent for every rotten thing she'd done in the past year. For stealing creative designs. For stealing customers. For sabotaging her business. For writing nasty articles. And for blackmail.

She stepped from the elevator. "Why now, what's going on down here. Some hanky panky?" she scolded. "I can't allow any of my workers to get involved with the hosts. Millicent, why don't you head upstairs? Now."

Teddy refused to let her go. "Move along, fatty. This doesn't concern you. I'll make sure you get a nice big tip."

"Why, young man. I'll have to talk with your mother about manners."

Teddy flashed the gun and placed the tip against Millicent's neck. "I'm not playing games. Where's Holly? Tell me now."

Millicent flashed her a desperate look.

"Fine," Holly said. "I'll tell you everything you need to know. First, let her go. She doesn't know anything."

"Prove it."

Holly didn't need to think twice. Painstakingly, she slid her fingers up into her hair and pulled off the wig and fake forehead. Then she peeled off the nose.

"Don't!" Millicent managed to say.

But this was Holly's mess. She needed to be the one to deal with Teddy and his family. With a shake, her red hair fell around her face. Teddy's eyes gleamed with excitement.

"That's more like it." He yanked Millicent off the freezer.

Holly caught her eyes and in Millicent she saw the friend underneath all the bad. "I forgive you."

Teddy knocked Millicent in the side of the head. She slumped to the floor.

"Why'd you do that?" Holly's temper flared.

"Can't have little mice running off to chit chat with anyone." He sidled up to Holly. "It's about time you showed up. I knew it was only a matter of time, darling."

Darling? He had to be kidding.

He glanced at his watch. "You were almost too late. But don't worry." He curled a finger around a lock of her hair. "We still have time."

Late? "Time for what?"

"Our wedding, of course."

Wedding? Impossible. Utterly ridiculous. "Don't you think we should have a date or several before making such a serious commitment?"

He flashed her a sardonic grin. "We're way past that stage, sweetheart. We have years of friendship. And you know—that's the best way to start off a marriage. Of course you know that. I'm not just marrying you for your looks." His eyes dropped to her cleavage. "Nice upgrade. Thanks, babe."

"They're fake," she stated, flatly.

"That's too bad." He waved the gun at her. "Time's a wasting."

There had never been a time where Holly wanted to stay in a basement. She never thought there'd be a time where she would think her childhood friend had turned into a complete psycho either. "Have you thought this through, Teddy?"

"That's Theodore," he said, coldly. "I'm running for mayor."

He really had lost it. What did he expect her to do? Stand by his side and support him after a fake wedding?

"Let's go." He forced her into the elevator.

"What about Millicent? Should we send one of my servants down to help her? You don't want a body count on your hands while running for office."

He slid the elevator door shut. "You're turning into a good wife already. Look at you." He pinched her cheek—a little too hard. "Wanting to protect my interests."

The elevator rose to the top, but he waited.

He pointed the gun at her neck and whispered, "One word and I won't hesitate."

Holly debated whether he'd pull the trigger. Her gut instinct said yes. For him to resort to kidnapping at this point, his plans must have veered out of control. Somehow, his brain had convinced him this logic worked in his grand plans.

She heard Charlene and Lindsey in the kitchen, loading more trays. She wanted to cough or scream or call out, but the metal against her neck, pointed up into her brain, kept her quiet. When they left the kitchen, Teddy peeked out. "All clear."

With a rough jerk, he pulled her through the kitchen and outside. They walked over the trampled flowerbeds and past the truck. Muffins!

"Should I get my purse?" She motioned to the truck. "Don't you want me to look pretty for our wedding?"

"Oh, how thoughtful." He caressed her cheek. "But you're a natural beauty."

"What about I.D. for the marriage license?"

"Fine. Go get it."

She walked to the truck and opened the door. She slid the purse over her shoulder. "Shh. Stay quiet, Muffins. Good dog."

Teddy led her to the six-car parking garage and pressed a button. The last one opened revealing a dark sedan with tinted windows. "All for you."

Holly climbed into the front seat. The first thing she noticed was a poofy bag in the backseat. At the bottom, white lacy fringes stuck out. A wave of dizziness washed through her. He had the dress?

That meant he had this whole thing planned out.

That meant he expected her to show up tonight.

That meant he'd been one step ahead of her the whole time.

19

ON THE ROAD, SHE couldn't help but glance at the dress. She'd certainly never been in this position before. Falling back on all her gained insight into psychopath killers—the best thing to do was play along and wait for a chance to escape. Maybe get some information from him at the same time.

"I see you noticed your dress." He reached over and laid a hand on her thigh, caressing her like she was a pet.

She tried not to tense up.

"Relax, Holly. This is the night we've been waiting for."

In the rearview mirror, Holly watched the lights of the house disappear, and they drove into the darkness. No one knew she left. But, Holly felt fairly confident Charlene would notice. She'd find Millicent, and then contact Trent. If that didn't work, she could always annul the marriage. Right?

The silence grew heavy. She followed instinct to get him talking. "So, Teddy, I mean Theodore. How have you been the past year I've been gone?"

His gaze flickered to hers. "I'll be honest. It's been difficult. Your parents left the company in a lurch. Your dad framed my father and made it look like he was stealing money from the company."

Did he really think that? Holly bit her lip. If that's what he thought, maybe she could play to his sense of justice. "What if it were true?" she asked softly.

He laughed, mocking and abrupt. "Oh, Holly. You're so innocent, so sweet. I'm trying to be nice here. I'm not your little friend who will do your bidding any more, or settle for scraps. We know your dad hid the information. We know you have it. I'll marry you. You'll share all your secrets with me."

Why the marriage? He could easily force the secrets without the matrimony.

"I know what you're thinking." He patted her leg. "See? I know you so well." He grinned. "We know where your parents are living, oblivious to everything."

He didn't need to say anymore. If she didn't cooperate, her parents could be hurt. Holly wondered if this was Teddy's plan, or his parents? His parents were intelligent and cunning, but somehow, she couldn't picture them diving off the deep end. She settled for staring out the window, as discouragement grew as thick as the darkness outside.

"Tell me about the cheesecake business. Was it everything you hoped for?"

Holly didn't feel like chatting, but she played along. She told him vague details and stories from the past year. Leaving out Trent. Her heart squeezed. Would she see him again? Would he know how much she loved him? Sure, she'd whispered it in the haze of sleep, but that was different than looking into his eyes, saying I love you, and sealing it with a kiss. Why had she wasted the precious time they had together? Of course, he'd understand. She could see that now.

A couple hours later, they pulled into a small, quaint chapel. Her heart sank. She didn't even know where they were. Teddy carried her dress with one hand and gripped her arm with the other. He pushed open the ancient doors into the musty lobby. The air was cold and dank. The stone chapel was beautiful. The stained glass windows, the wooden pews.

The swish of robes sounded in the darkness before the priest arrived, holding a candle. He had thinning white hair and an air of indifference about him as if he conducted fake weddings all the time. Holly wondered at the amount of money now padding his bank accounts.

"Welcome. I've prepared a room for you." He led them down a corridor.

When they entered, Holly gasped. Trays of fruit and cheese had been placed on a table, along with flutes of champagne. It turned her stomach. Teddy laid her dress over an antique armchair.

He caressed her cheek. "You'll make a beautiful bride." He dropped his hand, his gaze lingering on her mouth. He leaned in and kissed her. She didn't, couldn't, respond. "Come on now, darling. You can do better than that." He kissed her again.

She forced herself to return it, wanting to barf.

"Much better." At the door, he turned. "Might as well enjoy the wedding and the honeymoon. Mother always says, 'Attitude is everything.'"

When the door shut behind him, she sank into the chair, her nerves frayed, her body trembling, her mind and gut in turmoil. She opened her purse and hung onto Muffins as if he were the last friend she had.

She stayed that like for what felt like hours. Finally, Muffins whimpered.

"What is it, buddy?" He was trying to tell her something. "What?"

He whimpered again.

"I know." She sighed. "This isn't helping. I bet you're thinking, since when does Holly Hart let a situation get the best of her?"

She took a moment to let the words sink in. A knock on the door and a reminder from Teddy helped too. Slowly, she stood and examined the room. No large bay windows. Just two small squares near the ceiling that were practically ground level. She dragged the armchair—heavier than it appeared—to the window. With nothing to break the glass, she stripped off her shirt and wrapped it around her arm. Using her elbow, she banged on the window.

Nothing happened.

The movies made this look easy. She banged on it several times. Finally, a splinter. One last fear-fueled effort and the glass shattered. She lifted Muffins and let him slide through. "You go, buddy. See who you can find."

He gave her one last look and took off into the darkness.

"Holly?" Teddy asked, the latch on the door echoing.

"Wait!" Immediately, Holly stripped the rest of her clothes and stepped into the monstrosity of a dress with puffy sleeves, glitter, and beading everywhere. "You don't want to see the bride before the wedding. It's bad luck!"

Teddy eased off the door. "Five minutes. I'll be waiting."

Holly zipped the back of the dress the best she could. This wasn't quite like the wedding she'd always imagined. This wasn't anything like the dreams she and Teddy shared when they were young and innocent, when they talked about their futures. Where did that Teddy go? She didn't want to feel compassion, but years of parental pressure and failing to live up to expectations had taken their toll on him.

As she walked the corridor, her dress rustled. Tears burned hot. Would Muffins find anyone? She had to hold onto the hope that help was on the way. But as she stood at the end of the sanctuary, as she walked—as slowly as possible—down the aisle to the Wedding March, and when she stood before Teddy dressed in a tux, hope slipped away.

He squeezed her hand. "You look beautiful." He lifted her chin, forcing her to look at him. "I'll make you a deal."

She glanced at the priest, wondering how he could be letting this happen, and then at the door, hoping someone would burst through.

"Look at me." He gripped her chin forcefully. "No one is coming. I am your knight in shining armor. Are you ready to listen to my deal?"

"Yes," she forced out.

His expression softened. "I realize this isn't the ideal marriage. I'd rather the uneventful traditions too, because I know that's what you would want."

"We could still have that." She clung to the wisp of hope he'd offered.

"Sadly, no."

Her hopes crashed.

"But if you'll tell me where the evidence is hidden and it's confirmed, then I'll reconsider the unfortunate accident planned for you on our honeymoon. Maybe, if you cooperate, I'll let you live."

"I thought you loved me." That probably wasn't the most strategic dialogue, but this wasn't love. A person can't force love, just like Millicent couldn't with Trent. It just had to happen, along with honesty, hard work, and commitment. Somehow she'd forgotten the honesty part in the past few days.

"Just tell me."

Holly wished she knew. She'd assumed he took it with him. This piece of information would not make Teddy happy. "I don't know. And that's the truth."

He shrugged. "That's okay. No worries. We'll contact your parents and see if they'll tell us once they know you're in danger. Proceed," he ordered the priest.

It took that one second for Teddy to look at the priest, for Holly to stomp on his foot, and take off back down the aisle. But her dress was heavy and she wasn't used to moving in it.

Halfway to freedom, Teddy tackled her to the floor. She hit hard, the breath knocked from her chest. Seconds later, the gun jabbed into her back. "Let's try this again."

The door burst open.

20

WITH A SHARP YANK, Teddy pulled her to her feet.

In the time it took him to wrap his arm around Holly's neck, using her as a shield and a weapon, Trent had his gun trained on them.

Trent! She wanted to sob.

He stayed focused on Teddy.

Teddy pointed the gun in her neck and slowly moved back toward the pulpit. "So nice of you to join us but this is a closed ceremony."

"It's all over," Trent said, his voice calm and soothing like he was talking to a rabid dog. "We know everything. Chief Harrison has been arrested. We found the body of Senior Rumford in your freezer. Your parents are being questioned."

Teddy jerked. "What do you mean—the body?"

"Senior Rumford of Rumford & Rumford Law, has been missing since last week. Due to an anonymous call, we searched your parents' house. You're all under suspicion for murder and kidnapping charges."

In the next few seconds, Teddy must've figured out what happened. "Did you do this?" he hissed.

"I'm under suspicion of robberies so I thought I might as well live up to the rumors."

His grip tightened. "Leave now or I'll kill her." His voice turned to a screech. "I mean it."

Trent waited but when Teddy let off a warning shot at the floor by her feet and she screamed, Trent lowered his gun.

"I'm leaving." He eased backwards toward the exit.

"That's right. Like I said, this is a private ceremony."

Once again they were at the altar, except he didn't let go of her, arm still around her neck. "Proceed," he ordered.

"Are you quite sure?" the priest asked, wavering for the first time.

"I'm sure."

The priest proceeded as ordered, talking about nuptials and faith and commitment.

"Skip to the vows."

"Do you take this woman to be your lawfully wedded wife? In sickness—"

"I do."

"Do you take this man to be—"

The doors crashed open again. Men in uniform flooded the room. Shots rang out. Suddenly, Teddy grunted, his body jerked, and they fell forward. Holly hit the floor again, Teddy's body on top of her.

This time when her breath knocked from her chest, it was more than that. Pain seared her side. Had she been shot?

She drifted in and out of awareness as strong, safe arms scooped her up. "Stay with me, Holly, love of my life. Don't die on me now before I have a chance to tell you I want to spend the rest of my life with you." He ran with her out the door, the pain increasing with every jostle and jarring step. "Sorry, my love."

"Trent," she whispered.

He laid her on the backseat of his cruiser and slid in next to her. "The hospital and step on it."

"Right away." It sounded like Charlene.

The tears flowed. Trent smoothed her hair and wiped her tears. "What is it?"

"I'm sorry...should've told you."

"Shh. It's okay. Let's focus on you getting better first."

***

HOLLY MOVED IN THE bed. She cracked an eye to her surroundings, the machines, the bland wallpaper, and the beeping noises. Her vision cleared. "Mom? Dad?" she croaked.

They moved to the side of her bed. "Yes, sweetie. It's us. And we have so much to talk about."

"Not now though," her dad said. "We came as soon as we heard."

Holly's chest erupted and she blubbered, which caused more pain.

"Shh. We're here and we're not going anywhere."

"Teddy?"

"He was shot."

"His parents?"

"Arrested." He held her hand. "We have so much to tell you but that can wait. There's a young man waiting to see you. He was gracious enough to allow us time with you first."

"Just know," her mom said, "that all the bad guys have been caught. We are free to come out of hiding."

That information should make her happy, but instead it caused an ache. She didn't want to go back to stuffy parties and country clubs and rules. She didn't want to leave Fairview and her friends.

Her mom kissed her cheek. "Your life is your own, Holly, beautiful daughter of mine. You can make your own choices. You have our full support."

Then her dad kissed her cheek. "And that young man seems to be an upstanding guy." He winked. "I approve."

All too soon, they were gone, and Trent stood at the door. Her breathing grew shallow; she didn't know if it was due to the pain or nerves. His last words came back to her. Had she dreamed them?

He sat by her side and wove his fingers between hers. "Do you need anything? Water? Toast? I can call the nurse."

"I'm okay." She looked at him, his sandy hair that always seemed to need a cut, his soft, warm eyes, his smile that always cheered her up. He was a man of honor, a handsome man, a best friend.

"Will you marry me?" she blurted.

"What?"

Wait. What did she just say? "Never mind. It's too early. We have too much to work out. We'll probably be in counseling for months."

He stopped her with a kiss. "You stole my line. But yes, I'll marry you." He pulled a black box from his pocket. "I don't care that you were thinking about leaving and didn't talk to me about it. I understand. Sometimes we need space to think. And, I know you didn't want to put any of us in danger. Okay?"

"Okay," she whispered.

He took her hand. "Yes, I'll marry you." He slipped the diamond on her finger.

Holly was so shocked she couldn't feel the tremendous wave of happiness she should be feeling.

"And...with Chief Harrison out of the way, a position for Chief of Police has opened up in your town. But we can figure all that out later."

More tears flowed. Everything she could want. The best of both worlds. Her parents and Trent. The future held so much potential. But there was still one storyline left to close. "Millicent. I have to talk to Millicent."

Trent pulled away. "What?"

"Now."

"But my mom is waiting to see you."

"She'll understand. And I want you to stay too."

When Trent left to fetch Millicent, Holly closed her eyes, trying to absorb everything that was happening so fast. Her parents and her engagement and her near death. She remembered all the insights she'd had about Millicent.

They walked in together. Millicent held Muffins. She stood, shifting and petting him over and over. "The cops found him later."

"I love my dog, but I want to talk to you."

"Okay." Millicent laid Muffins next to her on the bed, then sat, not looking at Holly. "I'm sorry. For everything."

"I meant what I said. I forgive you. For everything."

Millicent looked up. "But why? I was horrible."

"Everyone needs second chances. You too. You have the potential to be a beautiful, kind, loving person. And I know you can do better. I have a proposition for you."

"What?" Millicent's eyes were brimming.

"I don't know where Trent and I will end up. But if we leave, or even if we stay, how would you and your father like to team up with me? Your dad can help out when he's able, because he's hurting more than he lets on. More than most people realize."

"How did you know?" Millicent whispered.

Holly winked. "Well, I've solved a mystery or two."

"I'm not going to hug you now, but when you're better, we're going to have a spa day." She blinked, almost as if she couldn't handle the love and acceptance. "And, oh, I have slips for you to sign so I can include your stories in my next mystery. Murder and Marriage. Or Catered to Death. I haven't decided."

Holly briefly closed her eyes. Exhaustion hit.

"I'll let you rest." Millicent leaned over and whispered, "Thank you."

After Millicent left, peace stole over Holly. She patted the bed. "Hold me?"

"I don't know about breaking the rules, Miss Hart. After all, I am an officer, sworn to uphold the law."

"We're engaged. Promise. I won't tell anyone."

Trent lay down next her and slid her into his embrace. Muffins curled between them. Holly rested her head against his chest, and for the first time, knew that whatever happened, she had her family and her friends, and she had Trent.

Maybe she was ready to live a normal life and hang up her detective hat.

Or maybe not.

THE END

About the Author

Laura Pauling writes about spies, murder, and mystery. She is the author of the Baron & Graystone Mysteries and the Holly Hart Cozy Mystery Series. She loves the puzzle of a whodunnit and witty banter between characters. In her free time, she likes to read, walk, bike, snowshoe, and spend time with family or enjoy coffee with friends. She writes to entertain, experience a great story, explore issues of friendship and forgiveness and... work in her jammies and slippers.

Visit Laura at http://laurapauling.com to sign up for her newsletter or send her a message through the contact tab. Or email her directly at laura@laurapauling.com.

Made in United States
Troutdale, OR
05/30/2024